THE RANLEIGH QUESTION

Lisa Boero

ISBN: 0998259918
ISBN 13: 9780998259918
Library of Congress Control Number: 2018902512
Nerdy Girl Press, Marshfield, WI

ALSO BY THE AUTHOR:

Murderers and Nerdy Girls Work Late

Bombers and Nerdy Girls Do Brunch

Kidnappers and Nerdy Girls Tie the Knot

"Kept afloat by a plucky heroine, like a yuppie version of Stephanie Plum."
Kirkus Reviews

The Richmond Thief, the first Lady Althea mystery

And **Hell Made Easy**, the first book in the
Trilogy from Hell

For all of the many fans of Lady Althea.
I had to keep the story going.

CHAPTER ONE

"I hope that Ranleigh lives up to expectations," Althea said, as the carriage bumped along the ruts of a country road.

"At least it will be a welcome respite for us both now that Arthur is back to his studies with Mr. Pellham. You know that you would be moped to death at Dettamoor Park without him," Jane replied.

"Or persecuted by Squire Pettigrew."

"You have only to tell Pettigrew that you are to marry the Duke of Norwich and he will leave off hounding you."

"But the engagement is to be kept secret, as you very well know, and telling Pettigrew would be like telling the world."

"I suppose so, but how can you decide if you and Norwich will suit if you do not spend the summer in his company?"

"He promises to come to Dettamoor when Cousin John and his wife visit, and I'm sure that several weeks within the confines of the Park will be more than enough to come to the point. Besides, like all dutiful sons, he must dance attendance on the Dowager Duchess, as she is still poorly in Bath."

Althea felt that no good could come of discussing the very precise permutations of the Gordian knot that her emotions had become, so she forcefully turned the conversation away from her romantic entanglements. "Who has Sir Neville invited to stay at Ranleigh with us? I am afraid with all of the excitement of having Arthur home again, I was not paying very close attention when you told me."

Jane smiled ruefully. "I had noticed. It is quite a diverse group. His letter said that he had invited Lord and Lady Pickney."

"That is delightful! I shall enjoy a sojourn with the endless gossip and lively wit of Lady Pickney, but I am surprised that Sir Neville should be able to get the very particular Pickneys to accept his invitation. Is he much acquainted with them?"

"No, but his letter hinted that, as you were to be one of the party, they deigned to accept the invitation. You must have made quite an impression on Lady Pickney."

"Honesty is such a refreshing quality. And she was right about Cousin Charles. He was like a fox let loose in the hen house. If only I had paid attention to her!"

"The less said about our dead cousin, the better, I think."

Althea shuddered. "I am in complete agreement. Who else comes to Ranleigh?"

"Lord and Lady Batterslea are also invited. She is the celebrated beauty, if you remember."

"I know I have seen her – the tall blonde with the alabaster skin and sleepy eyes – but cannot ever remember speaking to her."

"I don't count that as a loss. I have spoken to her several times and don't rate her conversation all that highly. Then again, she is very young, and so bound to be a little foolish," Jane said.

"Spoken with the voice of experience."

Jane ignored her. "Then there is Mr. Smithson, who was that funny little man with the loud waistcoats who always hung about looking sulky and overwrought. Sir Neville tells me that he is the uncontested leader of the dandy set, so I suppose that must count for something. Between you and me, however, I think Smithson must have invited himself, as I can't see Sir Neville choosing him as a boon companion."

Althea, who credited Sir Neville's desire to marry the level-headed Jane with making Sir Neville considerably less silly than he had been before, held her tongue. If Sir Neville had chosen to associate with a set of very foolish men in the past, she was certainly not in a position to comment or to judge him.

Jane continued on. "Also joining the group are Mr. and Mrs. Gregson, who are an older couple from somewhere up north. And Baron Tunwell, who was that dour man we once sat next to at the theater. I gather he was a friend of Sir Neville's father, or uncle, or something. Lord Tunwell, the Gregsons and Lord and Lady Batterslea have been to

Ranleigh before, so I am hopeful that they will turn out to be a pleasant and welcoming party."

Althea smiled. "I am sure Sir Neville will do all in his power to make it so."

The lane to Ranleigh turned to the left and widened into a more tolerable road. Althea could see the beginning of what looked to be the grounds of the estate, and just beyond the next curve, the start of the ornamental gardens for which Ranleigh was justifiably famous.

Althea hoped the sojourn in Ranleigh would help her to settle on the right path. She needed time and distance to decide if the feelings she harbored for the duke were merely a combination of lust, produced by the skills of a man well versed in the arts of dalliance, and gratitude for saving her from a fate worse than death at the hand of her cousin. If so, the match would not suit. However, if her feelings portended the kind of mutual regard essential for a fulfilling marriage, then she might look forward to a happy union, which was the only kind that could tempt her as a wealthy, independent widow.

And there was another matter that troubled her. She had found herself strangely attracted to the duke's brother, Lord George Verlyn, but she couldn't tell if this attraction was real or simply a mild flirtation ballooned out of proportion by her vivid imagination when she thought that he was the Richmond Thief. It was all such a distressing muddle.

"The gardens should be at their most delightful this time of year, " Jane said, as if to force the subject away from painful memories. "And there are streams and a large ornamental pond that Sir Neville had dredged. I am told that the fishing is quite good, if one is inclined to be an angler."

"You seem to know a great deal about the house. Perhaps this visit will convince you once and for all to become its mistress."

"Sir Neville may have had such an object in mind," Jane admitted.

"And if Ranleigh is such a beautiful place, I wonder that your parents did not look upon Sir Neville's suit with favor in your first London season?"

"It was so heavily mortgaged at the time. The Tabards did not have a feather to fly with back then. It was only after a black sheep uncle who had run off to make his fortune in the East Indies died and left that fortune to Sir Neville that he was able to set the property to rights. That was some years after my parents had died, and I was ensconced at Dettamoor Park once again."

"There is still time, dear Jane. If Dettamoor Park will decide my future with Norwich, Ranleigh may yet decide yours with Sir Neville."

Jane sighed. "That is the Ranleigh question, I suppose."

"In any case, the grounds should supply me with all that I need of natural wonders for a clever scientific paper. I have been fretting over what is to be the topic of my next monograph for the Royal Society. It must be as novel as the last one was."

Althea had faced a hostile reception by the all-male Royal Society until she had submitted her work under the guise of her late husband's studies, posthumously compiled by his devoted wife. She hoped to continue this ruse until such time as her work could be properly recognized, thus allowing her to take her rightful place among the scientists of her day.

Her first monograph, describing the Trent method for determining the amount of time a cadaver had been left outside based upon the stages of the insects found upon it, had been widely acclaimed, not only because of its scientific merit, but also because of its practical application to crime detection. Mr. Read, the Magistrate of Bow Street, had been particularly effusive in his praise and commissioned Althea to prepare training materials for his Principal Officers, the only persons in London employed solely to solve crimes. It would be marvelous to hit upon just such a meritorious and useful study once again, but so far, no idea had yet occurred to Althea.

Jane shook her head. "I am sure that you will be able to make a study of every creepy crawly thing your heart desires. And if no new thing presents itself, you have some notes my brother left to compile."

In extremis only, Althea thought, but she hesitated before replying. It would not do to tell Jane just how much she worried about her scientific projects. Jane had a tendency to fret over Althea's unorthodox habits and their potential effect on Althea's social standing. It was ridiculous, but endearing. Besides, Jane needed all of her attention focused on the problem of becoming Sir Neville's wife.

"You are probably right, dear Jane. I'm sure I shall be able to pull something together. Ah, I think I see Sir Neville waving to us."

They were met at the door by Sir Neville himself, round and red-cheeked in the summer sun. He hurried up to the carriage. "My dear Lady Trent and Miss Trent, how delighted I am to welcome you to Ranleigh. I trust the journey was not too fatiguing?"

"No, Sir Neville, you find us ready for any amusement Ranleigh shall offer," Althea replied. "We have taken the trip in easy stages so as not to exhaust the horses."

He handed her out of the carriage and then turned a smiling face to Jane. "Miss Trent, I have long wished to introduce you to Ranleigh. Welcome."

Jane looked slightly uncomfortable, but managed to reply, "The pleasure is all mine, Sir Neville."

Sir Neville gave orders for their carriage to be sent back to the stables and for John, the coachman, to be accommodated. Miss Dorkins, the elderly abigail employed by the Dettamoor ladies, also alighted and was cordially offered refreshment in the kitchen, while Jane and Althea were offered a cup of tea and some plum cakes in the rose drawing room. Sir Neville informed them that a picnic nuncheon was to be served in an hours' time in the rose garden. The baron, Mr. Smithson, and Mr. And Mrs. Gregson were the only guests to have already arrived, but Lord and Lady Pickney were expected later that afternoon.

"The rose garden at Ranleigh is famous, I understand, for the variety and beauty of its roses," Jane remarked, in between sips of fragrant tea. "Which of the Knights of Tabard planted it?"

"Sir Walter Tabard, the fourth Knight, first planned the gardens at the time of the second King Charles, but they weren't brought to their present state until very recently. I have undertaken a great deal of new work in the grounds, including an ornamental pond that I think heightens the untamed beauty of Ranleigh quite delightfully."

"We shall hope to have a complete tour," Jane said.

"Yes, and the pond as well. My late husband had thought to have one dug at the Park, but never realized that plan." Althea said.

"But of course. I shall be honored to take you myself."

After tea, Jane and Althea were shown to their rooms by the housekeeper, Mrs. Howell. She was a kindly woman who clearly took great pride in unveiling the stately apartments lately refurbished by their host in the classical style. Jane's room was at the middle of the long hall, with Althea's next to hers, connected by a small anteroom where the housekeeper had made up a bed for Miss Dorkins.

When Jane and Althea were left alone to freshen up before they joined Sir Neville and the other guests out in the garden, Althea said, "Well, he has good taste in furniture, in any case. I had expected just the sort of heavy oak timeworn pieces we have at the Park, not the latest fashion in Grecian settees."

"The rooms are quite lovely, I admit. Sir Neville has always had an artistic eye."

"Perhaps that is why he is in love with you."

"I hardly think so."

Their trunks arrived along with a slightly frazzled Miss Dorkins. "Oh, my dear Lady Trent and Miss Trent, I'm so sorry it took me so long. Here, let me help you both out of your traveling dresses and into something fit to be seen. Oh, I do hope that the blue muslin hasn't been crushed beyond all repair!"

Althea laughed. "Calm yourself, Miss Dorkins. We shall select another dress if that one is wrinkled. It is just the

Gregsons and the baron, after all. I don't suppose they care what sort of dress I wear to an al fresco nuncheon, as I am not very well acquainted with any of them."

"You forget, there is Mr. Smithson, as well. But I think he is more likely to be preoccupied with his own dress rather than with ours. Dandies usually are," said Jane.

"Yes, so you see, Miss Dorkins, there is absolutely no reason to fear that you will disgrace yourself when I appear. Besides, I have a great deal of faith in your ability to make a silk purse out of a sow's ear."

Miss Dorkins tut-tutted and set about pulling Jane and Althea out of their traveling dresses. She then fussed about unpacking the trunks, putting their clothes to rights, and cosseting them like a mother hen. Finally, she had them dressed, Althea in the blue muslin and Jane in a flower printed muslin that was very becoming indeed. Althea and Jane let her corral them for a final inspection, and then a servant came to guide them to the garden. As they crossed into the hall, Miss Dorkins reached up and adjusted Althea's straw bonnet. It was trimmed with blue satin ribbon and tied roguishly under Althea's ear.

"Colors do so favor you, Lady Trent. I am glad your mourning time is over," she said.

Althea, who did miss the practicality of her previous black dresses, merely smiled and led Jane down the hall.

CHAPTER TWO

M r. Smithson was the only guest seated at the small table set out in the middle of a fragrant swath of red rose bushes at the center of the rose garden. He was a small, youngish man with a very long neck wreathed entirely by the tight linen fabric of an intricate cravat. His collar points were so high and so stiff with starch that he seemed to have some difficulty in turning his head, and so he always seemed to view his companions out of the corner of his eye, like a fish. He wore a brocade waistcoat of startling pattern and an extremely tight coat with obviously padded shoulders. Around his neck hung a long black ribbon, with an intricate gold quizzing glass attached at the end. This he raised to one eye as the ladies approached and then, dropping it with a practiced air, he stood and bowed to them.

"Mr. Smithson at your service, Lady Trent and Miss Trent."

Jane and Althea responded with inclinations of the head. "Pleased to meet you, Mr. Smithson," they replied in turn.

"Forgive the informality of the introduction. Our good host was called away to attend to Mr. Gregson with some trifling matter. Lady Trent and Miss Trent, I am delighted to make your acquaintance at last. I have heard much, but let me say that the reality surpasses all of the rumors."

"Very pretty, sir," Althea said.

Jane followed with a hard look and then seated herself on the other side of the table.

Althea took the chair held by Mr. Smithson. "The reality of the Ranleigh rose garden also surpasses any previous description. I don't think I have ever seen such a profusion of blooms or such a variety of color. Are you as fond of gardens as Sir Neville, Mr. Smithson?"

"Can't say as I have much experience with them, Lady Trent. My family is from the north, where such profusions of greenery are harder to produce."

"Where in the north?" Jane said.

"Yorkshire, so you can see why I have escaped to the Metropolis. Sir Neville tells me that Dettamoor Park is in Somerset."

"Yes," Jane replied, and then, turning her head, she added, "and here is Sir Neville."

Sir Neville arrived, his countenance even more florid than before and his corsets creaking in time with his steps. He mopped his damp brow with a perfumed handkerchief and said breathlessly, "Mr. And Mrs. Gregson will join us presently. And I saw Lord Tunwell this morning at breakfast, so I'm sure he will join us as well. May I offer you some refreshment while we wait? Some lemonade or perhaps a mild claret? I shall have them brought directly."

"I am quite refreshed enough with the tea you have previously offered, but perhaps you might show us some of this lovely garden while we wait?" Jane said.

"But of course, Miss Trent." He motioned for a footman who had followed him out and gave him instructions to come and find them when Mr. or Mrs. Gregson emerged from the house. Then he held out his arm to Jane."

Mr. Smithson stood. "Perhaps, Lady Trent, you would join me in taking a turn about the garden as well?"

"With pleasure."

The four set out, but Althea soon took the opportunity of separating herself from Jane and Sir Neville. When they were out of earshot, she steered Mr. Smithson away from the roses. "We must give Cupid his full share of opportunity," she said in a conspiratorial whisper. "Come, I have a great desire to see the pond Sir Neville has spoken of. Do you know which direction we should go?"

Mr. Smithson pointed to the left. "It is beyond those trees."

They walked in silence for several moments and then Mr. Smithson said, "So you've a desire to see old Sir Neville leg shackled at last? What devilish plots you women hatch."

"Not devilish, merely practical. Sir Neville has been pining for Jane since her first season, and I mean to see him get his wish, if I can." She paused and looked at him archly. "Do you have a problem with matrimony, Mr. Smithson?"

"No indeed, not that I am in the petticoat line myself, but I'm sure it does other men no end of good."

"Then we are agreed." They came to a group of trees and passed through onto a close-cropped lawn with ornamental plantings. "I see the pond up ahead. Look at how lovely the water shimmers in the light. Come, perhaps we shall be lucky enough to see a frog or two."

"A frog?" Mr. Smithson's face contorted in a grimace. "Whatever should we want to see a frog for?"

Althea smiled at his discomposure. "I take it you are not a naturalist?"

Smithson shook with revulsion, "Good heavens, no!"

"Then I promise not to press you into service. Sir Arthur Trent was quite enamored of scientific pursuits, and has infected me with a similar affliction. I'm afraid that once you acquire a desire to study the natural world, you can never quit it, no matter the consequences."

"What an extraordinary state of affairs, Lady Trent. I had no idea that Sir Neville kept such interesting company."

Althea wasn't sure if he meant to offend her or not, but decided to disarm him in any case. "We are of the same mind then. It was just what I thought when I knew you to be one of the party."

Smithson smiled, acknowledging the hit. "I begin to understand why London took you to its heart. You were made for better things than Somerset."

Althea smiled innocently. "I cannot imagine why."

They reached the edge of the pond and Althea paused, cautioning Mr. Smithson not to speak. There was a chirping sound coming from deep inside a stout stand of rushes.

Althea bent down and then pried the rushes apart, revealing a small pale green frog.

"See. This one makes a sound that is almost bird-like."

Smithson moved only slightly closer. "How enterprising. Seems like a sprightly little fellow."

At that moment, the frog decided to leap off his present perch down into the marshy water below. The sudden movement made Smithson start. "Good heavens!"

Althea laughed. "They are very quick but quite harmless. Do not be afraid, Mr. Smithson."

"No indeed, I am not afraid, I assure you. Is Dettamoor Park quite filled with frogs?"

Althea stepped back. "There are many by the little brook that runs through the meadow. My husband did a study of toads once, so I was often following him around the countryside making sketches."

"How delightful that must have been," Smithson said without conviction. "As much as I am thrilled by these stories of pastoral bliss, perhaps we should return to the rose garden?"

Althea sighed. Mr. Smithson was clearly not fit for scientific investigation, but it was such a lovely pond that she hated to quit it. Then her eye caught sight of something strange in amongst the bull rushes, some twenty feet from where they stood. It looked like a blue piece of fabric, submerged in the water. Althea pointed it out to Smithson. "What is that?"

"Appears to be a piece of fabric, perhaps torn in passing by the bull rushes."

"But who would be walking that close to the pond?" Althea came closer and Smithson followed, albeit with an air of reluctance.

"It really is of no matter," he said. "Come, Lady Trent."

Althea ignored him and approached the spot. As she did so, she had a sinking feeling. There seemed to be a form under the fabric. She pulled away at the vegetation with her hands. Yes, there was no doubt the blue was part of a gentleman's coat, and it appeared that the gentleman was still attached!

CHAPTER THREE

"Help me, Mr. Smithson! Someone has drowned in the pond!"

Smithson turned a further shade of gray and stepped back. "Oh, my dear lord, what a horror! Come away, Lady Trent, I beg of you!"

Althea went into the water without a second thought, but found that it was far deeper than she had anticipated. Her foot slipped on the muddy bottom and she grabbed a fistful of reeds to steady herself. "No point in saying that now. If you won't help me, then go find someone who will. Hurry!"

Smithson paused a moment, seeming to debate the wisdom of proving his manhood through assistance or running away, but his manhood must have held second place to the fear that the sight of a dead body might prove overwhelming to his delicate sensibilities. "I shall be right back,

Lady Trent. I beg you would come away until others may help you."

Althea ignored him and began frantically pulling at the reeds and tugging at the body to disengage it enough to push it onto the grass of the bank. Unfortunately, he was a large man and Althea couldn't manage to pull him free enough to get a good look at his face. She didn't recognize the blue coat, but the fabric was a fine woven wool, indicating that the man was most likely a gentleman. But who? She felt down along the back of the victim and over to the side submerged in water where a coat pocket would be. She pulled out a watch, now covered with mud and bracken, on a fine gold chain. Nothing to give her a clue as to the identity of the body except a fob in the shape of a cylinder. It was inscribed in some fashion, but Althea could not tell with the mud. She tried to wipe the mud away, but the fob broke off the chain instead. She tucked it inside her chemise at the bust line of her dress, as otherwise, there seemed no way to prevent its being lost in all the rest of the watery mud.

Then she heard Jane's voice behind her. "My word, Althea, what are you up to now?"

Althea turned and saw Sir Neville and Jane running, as best either could, towards her, several large footmen and one very bedraggled Mr. Smithson in tow. Althea hastily stuffed the watch back in the pocket. "Nothing you wouldn't have done, dear Jane. But now that reinforcements are arrived, I shall surrender the field. Some poor soul has drowned and I was trying to get him out."

Althea waded back out of the pond, aware for the first time how much of a sodden muddy mess she must appear to all. She could feel Jane's disapproval without even having to look. Instead, of worrying about propriety, however, she focused on directing the footmen.

When they had pulled the body free and laid it on its back on the bank, Althea squatted down beside it. It was apparent that the drowning was a recent occurrence because the face was not bloated or misshapen and rigor mortis had not set in. However, the lips were pulled back from the teeth and the eyes were wide open, staring blankly at the sky.

Sir Neville came up behind her. "Why, it is Lord Tunwell!" he cried, "Whatever could have happened?"

"Perhaps he slipped on the bank and fell in," Jane said.

"Perhaps," Althea replied. She scanned the body. No blood was mixed in with the mud at his chest, thus eliminating the possibility of a stabbing or gunshot wound. The face appeared to have been scratched and the hands also, but those could have been made trying to break free of the reeds. Althea stood up and walked over to where they had pulled him out. Like many ornamental structures, the pond showed evidence of having been gouged out of the earth all at once. Instead of the sloping depths of more natural formations, the pond was waste deep as soon as one stepped off the bank. The reeds were thick just where the baron had gone in, so it might have been difficult to climb back out. However, in Althea's experience, one didn't usually fall face first into the water with one's eyes open unless one had been pushed. It was all very puzzling, especially since the baron was still young enough to have made an effort to save himself.

"My dear Lady Trent, do come back into the house. You are soaked through and will certainly catch your death of cold," Sir Neville said, snapping Althea out of her reverie.

"Yes," Jane added. "Come Althea, we must get you changed immediately. I'm sure the gentlemen can take care of poor Lord Tunwell."

Althea took one last look at the body, committing as many details to memory as possible, and then turned back with Jane. When they were out of earshot, Althea said, "'l will have no lectures on the propriety of going into ponds to retrieve dead bodies, Jane. One must do what one must in the moment."

Miss Dorkins was as aghast as Jane might have been had Althea allowed her to express her sentiments. However, in Miss Dorkins case, it wasn't so much Althea's person as the blue muslin that warranted her deepest sighs. "And such a lovely shade of blue it was, too! Lady Trent, I am most disheartened, for the yellow or the figured muslin dresses are not nearly so fine and the blue just set off your ladyship's complexion."

"I am sure I shall survive the loss with equanimity," Althea replied, "but if you would be so kind as to have hot water brought up, I should very much like a bath."

"Oh yes, why of course I shall see to it personally, never fear." And with that she scurried off to secure a tub and some pails of hot water.

Jane was harder to fob off. "Now that Dorkins is gone, you can tell me what made you dive into the pond like a lunatic."

"I am such a trial for you, aren't I, Jane? And I had even drawn Mr. Smithson away for the sole purpose of giving you a moment with Sir Neville, too! It was unpardonable of me to cause such a scene and take you from your romantic idyll."

"Fiddle. Sir Neville was merely showing me some roses. But you still haven't answered my question. Why couldn't you have waited for help like a sensible person? The poor baron was not going to run away from you."

"Because I am not a sensible person. Do you think he actually fell into the pond? For my part, I can't believe it to be true."

"Be that as it may, that is the story we are going to stick to until another comes along."

"I suppose you are right, and yet it seems very odd."

"Althea, please."

CHAPTER FOUR

Two hours later, Althea had finally sent Miss Dorkins on her way with a promise to lie down for an hour in order to calm her nerves. Said nerves were entirely in Miss Dorkins' imagination because Althea felt remarkably well after a bath. It was amazing how a little hot water and a fragrant bar of fine French soap could entirely change one's outlook on the day. Althea sat by the fire in a silk dressing gown, her long hair loose around her shoulders, and pulled out a letter that had just arrived from the Duke of Norwich.

That gentleman had been exceedingly regular in his correspondence, and Althea had to admit that she looked forward to receipt of such letters. It was apparent, however, that despite the notable rumors regarding his previous entanglements, he had not spent much time composing those delicate missives Althea imagined other women might require. It was fortunate, therefore, that Althea had no experience with such florid language. She was quite content to receive word of his daily activities and his thoughts on politics, society, and any other topic that seemed to occupy his mind.

Every now and then, however, he would throw in a blunt phrase that made a blush work its way up her cheek. She had to admit that, even though she was a rational creature, she rather enjoyed the duke's admiration. It was certainly a novel experience as Sir Arthur had never been one for fulsome compliments.

The letter that Althea now opened followed the previous ones in that it began with an amusing description of his present sojourn in Bath, accompanied by a reminder that Althea had promised to come to the point within six months.

And, by my calculations, more than two months has now passed, shortening my torment by fully one third. I will confess, my dear Althea, that I find that time has not eased the burden. Trust me when I say that I have never felt such trepidation as I feel when I think that you may perhaps have changed your mind and now mean to send me away. Although it is likely a result of my sojourn with the aged and infirm set of friends my mother keeps in Bath, I have need of your reassurance that you will be firm and tell me straight away should you not feel that you can bring yourself to marry me. I have not explained matters to my mother for fear to break her heart as well as mine should you decide against me, but she is certainly aware that I have been much in your company.

In keeping with the family theme, I was happy to receive your description of your brief visit to Dettamoor Park and the much-desired reunion with your son. How is his progress? If he is anything like his parents, I am sure he will be one of the most brilliant men of his generation. I hesitate to ask, because I assume one does not like to discuss one's intimate thoughts with one's children, but have you perhaps mentioned my existence to him? I will admit that if you have, it will give me some reason to hope.

I am sorry that this letter is such a tangle of wondering thoughts, but such is the state of mind my attachment to you has wrought. In short, Bath is a lesson to me. Time is not our friend, Althea, and if we are to be happy, we should not delay. Write to me as soon as you are able.
Yours,
N.

Althea folded the letter, unsure of exactly how to reassure Norwich without completely capitulating to his demands for an immediate answer. It was hard to decide what was best. She had indeed mentioned the duke to her son, but only as much as young Arthur needed to know in order to prepare for his visit. As she stared absently around the room, her eyes caught sight of the cylinder fob, perched on the edge of her desk. She got up and retrieved it. Once she had dressed, she must find a way to return it to the pocket of the corpse.

Through the wonderful penchant of Miss Dorkins for servant gossip, and her willingness to interrupt Althea's quiet contemplation of the bath in order to relay the story, Althea knew that they had taken the body to a makeshift table in one of the little-used sitting rooms in the old wing of the house. A messenger had also been sent to London express to the home of Lord Tunwell's nephew and heir, Mr. Cruikshank.

Althea noted on closer examination that the fob was of an unusual design; worked all over with a pattern of ivy. It seemed solid, but there appeared to be a join that might indicate a hollow core. *If I were to hide something, this would be the perfect place*, she thought. Her curiosity now fully captured, she ran her fingernail along the seam, but it didn't come open. Perhaps on one of the circular ends. She probed with her fingers, pushing and pulling until she twisted one end and finally the cylinder popped open and fell with a clatter to the floor, revealing a tight white roll of paper inside. The fob was so cunningly wrought that, despite its owner's watery death, the paper was completely dry.

She picked the cap up and then pried the roll out of the tube with a pen knife. She carefully unrolled that paper and held it up to the fire in order to make out the very small handwriting. It looked to be the lines of a map of some sort and the word *Al Andalus* at the top. *How very strange*, she said to herself. *What could it mean?* She knew from her own study of history that *Al Andalus* was the Moorish name for Spain, but beyond that, the name conveyed no other information.

After staring at the paper for some time, she put it aside and set herself to the task of answering Norwich. She went over to the writing desk and, after starting several letters meant to convey to him that her sojourn had been uneventful, she pulled a piece of paper towards her and started anew.

> *My dear Sir,*
> *Thank you for your last letter. I was highly entertained by your observations on the present society at Bath. I hope your mother improves in health and spirits. Something of a most alarming nature has occurred here at Ranleigh. Rest assured that I am well, but one of our guests is not. Lord Tunwell was discovered this afternoon drowned in the pond under circumstances that I cannot but think are suspicious. I dare not say more until I have investigated further. I will write again with more particulars as soon as I am able.*
> *Yours most cordially,*
> *Althea*

She sealed the letter and addressed it to Norwich's lodgings in Bath. She then rang the bell and asked the maid who arrived to please make sure that it was franked for inclusion with the other letters leaving Ranleigh for the rest of England. She tucked the scrap of paper and Norwich's letter into the packet of his other letters, tied the whole with a ribbon and placed it in the armoire amongst her linen chemises. Then she put the fob back together and slipped it into her reticule.

When Miss Dorkins arrived to dress her for dinner, Althea selected a pale yellow satin dress that Madame Longet had made up for her right before that unfortunate incident with Cousin Charles. She had worn it one evening at Norwich House and the duke had paid her a most extravagant compliment. Or at least, extravagant for him.

"That color favors you, Althea; like the bloom of a primrose," he'd said.

It was, in the grand scheme of things, quite an honor. And Althea felt its full effect, but her blush of pleasure was tinged with just that edge of panic at the thought of belonging so completely once again to a man. Widowhood had given her an intoxicating taste of freedom that she was loathe to part with, however tempting the alternative. Compliments via the distance of a letter were so much more agreeable.

Jane entered the room just as Miss Dorkins fastened the last button up the back of the dress. "So, you are feeling better?"

"I am quite recovered. It is amazing what hot water can do for the soul. My father, as you know, was a great proponent of a hot bath as often as could be managed."

Jane nodded. "It is a good thing you are so recovered, for I fear it is not so with the other occupants of the house. The Pickney's carriage just pulled into the drive and Sir Neville is terrified of what Lady Pickney will say when she finds out about the baron's untimely end. The Gregsons are already hinting that it would be best to leave, and Mr. Smithson retired to his room complaining of a severe headache and hasn't been seen since. This must be the worst start of any house party I have ever heard of."

"Poor Sir Neville! But surely Lady Pickney is not so mean as to blame Sir Neville for what happened to Lord Tunwell. Let us go down and see what assistance we can render."

CHAPTER FIVE

The Dettamoor Park ladies arrived to find that the death of Lord Tunwell had not rendered the house party unworthy in Lady Pickney's eyes. Althea found her in the rose drawing room, seated by the fire, sipping a cup of tea while the house servants dealt with her very substantial luggage.

"Ah, my dear Lady Trent and Miss Trent, I find that we have not only arrived inconveniently right before dinner, but also to sad tidings. It is too bad. My lord has gone off to render some assistance to Sir Neville, and dinner is to be pushed off an hour, but do come sit down and tell me all about it. We must console our loss with the balm of conversation, as we women are wont to do. Besides, I find the country so free from delicious gossip, that I am quite at a loss to amuse myself. Would you like some tea?"

Jane declined, but Althea realized that she was suddenly both hungry and thirsty, so she poured herself a cup and sat down across from Lady Pickney. Lady Pickney had once been quite a beauty, but a happy marriage and many offspring had left her plump and plain. She still retained her sharp wit, however, and had acquired a reputation for frankness that was rightly to be feared. Fortunately, she and Althea had an easy understanding, and so Althea had no hesitation in laying the outline of the events of the afternoon before her.

"It is odd that a man so careful as Lord Tunwell should walk so close to the pond," Lady Pickney said, after she had heard the whole tale.

"Was he careful?" Jane said. "I'm afraid we didn't know him very well at all."

"At least when it came to money and dress and friends. And really, there isn't much else for a man to be extravagant about, is there? Unless you include women, but I never heard one breath of scandal, and I count myself tolerably well informed." She paused and then shook her head, "No, nothing extravagant for Lord Tunwell, and the dullest set of friends you would ever want to meet. It was a great surprise to me when Sir Neville told me that the baron would make one of the party. I didn't think that they were very well acquainted. I mean, the Duke of York would never be caught associating with such a man, and we know that Sir Neville is his great friend. Then again, one never knows what a host might be thinking when he sets out to compose a guest list."

"Lord Tunwell was a friend of Sir Neville's uncle, I believe," Jane said.

"Ah, that explains that."

"Lord Tunwell was a widower of long standing, I am told," Althea said. "Did you know his late wife?"

"I met her once or twice, but I can't remember that she entertained much. She was a Doncaster and very proud like the rest of them, so perhaps my ton wasn't good enough." Lady Pickney laughed without malice. "A very noble family, the Doncasters, but entirely without means."

"But I understood that Lord Tunwell was a man of some property," Jane said.

"Lord Tunwell inherited a vast sum of money from a cousin, who made his fortune abroad in some sort of business venture. It was all very secret and so not likely to be from reputable sources. In any case, Lord Tunwell had got the money by the time he married Livia Doncaster, so I don't suppose it mattered that she hadn't any money. I am told that her family was happy for the fortune, but not for the potential scandal behind it. They say it was a love match, but I have trouble imagining the steady baron falling hopelessly in love. His very caution would preclude it."

"Who knows what lies in the hearts of men?" Althea replied.

Lady Pickney smiled. "I should remember that I am speaking with two ladies who have been, if reports are correct, recently struck by Cupid's arrows, and should hold my tongue on the subject of love."

Althea laughed. "For my part, I disclaim any knowledge of that winged visitor. Jane, you may answer as you please."

"I have no particular comment to make," Jane said, with some asperity.

Lady Pickney clucked her tongue. "I see I shall have to be devious in my methods if I am the extract the whole story. Suffice it to say that the attentions of the Duke of Norwich and Sir Neville have not gone unnoticed in polite society.

I hate to be the bearer of unpleasant tidings, but they are laying bets at the gentlemen's clubs that two such notable bachelors shall be caught before next season begins."

"Men can be odious creatures, can't they?" said Althea. "But tell me more of Lord Tunwell. Word has been sent to his nephew and heir. I assume that that gentleman will inherit quite a fortune?"

"Yes, the baron certainly hasn't spent what he received. Cruikshank is another matter, I'm afraid. I don't know that you and Miss Trent will have met him. He spends most of his time pursuing gentlemen's amusements in locations that ladies of reputation are not likely to frequent."

"Like his father, then," Jane replied.

Lady Pickney nodded. "I'm sure you remember as well as I do, Miss Trent, the scandal it was when the senior Mr. Cruikshank ran off with Dorothea Doncaster. How such a steady girl could have fallen for the wiles of Mr. Cruikshank, I shall never understand."

"Cruikshank was prodigiously handsome, as I remember," Jane said, "and rumor had it that Lady Doncaster kept her daughter so tied to apron strings that the poor girl was bound to fall for the first rake who offered to break her out of the house."

Lady Pickney smiled. "You are exactly right, Miss Trent. I had heard much the same story. It just goes to show that girls must have a taste of freedom before they are brought out. Otherwise, they rate freedom too highly."

Althea was about to reply, but then held her tongue. Likely Lady Pickney would not relish Althea's defense of freedom.

Lady Pickney continued on. "Girls should be taught to understand marriage as a serious subject and not be swayed by good looks and a dashing manner. Lady Trent and I had a similar conversation the evening of Lady Shirling's masquerade. Of course, I didn't know it was Lady Trent at the time. That beetle costume was quite arresting, Lady Trent. I don't know how you managed to come up with such an original idea. Those of us who stayed with mythological or literary figures were cast in the shade completely."

"As you may know, I have a particular interest in the natural world, and I had my husband's manuscript about *Dermestes trentatus* quite on my mind at the time."

"I am sorry we missed your lecture at the Royal Society. My husband tells me that it made quite an impression in scientific circles and put fools like that Randolph Booth in their places with their esoteric scientific studies. I ask you, who wants to learn about subjects that will never do anyone any good? Practical application of science is what is needed in our modern times. Sir Arthur Trent clearly understood that."

Althea felt a twinge of resentment that her work should have to be attributed to her late husband, but quickly quelled it. One day the truth would come out. "Thank you. I am very grateful to the Society for the opportunity to publish my husband's work posthumously. It was his great wish to see it done."

Lady Pickney nodded in approval and appeared as if she would have commented further, but at that moment, the door opened and a liveried servant informed her that her room was ready. Lady Pickney got up. "Now I must leave you to your own amusements, and I promise I shall not make you wait for your dinner more than is strictly necessary."

CHAPTER SIX

An hour later, the party assembled again in the great
dining room of Ranleigh. Both the Gregsons and Mr.
Smithson made their appearance, and so it was to be assumed that the original arrangements held firm. Sir Neville
arranged the guests by rank for the procession into dinner,
as was proper, but Althea could see that it cost him some not
to take Jane's arm, for he hovered by her side rather longer
than was necessary. Althea and Jane, ranking lower down
in the scheme of nobility, ended up with the Gregsons and
Mr. Smithson. The Gregsons appeared to be somewhat older than Sir Neville and Jane. They were a well-bred, elegant
couple, the kind of people forever invited to the most exclusive parties because they filled in a guest list without ever
outshining the hosts. In looks, they were unremarkable as
well, except that Mrs. Gregson had come from Scottish nobility and bore the sign of that lineage in her red hair and

fair complexion. They were dressed nicely but not in a way to bring attention to themselves, and there was nothing of the dandy in Mr. Gregson's distinguished good looks.

After some minor commentary on the excellence of the soup, Althea took the conversational plunge and said to Mr. Gregson, who was seated to her right, "Such a sad state we find ourselves in this evening. Although I was not very well acquainted with Lord Tunwell, his untimely death is most distressing."

"Yes, I'm sure we all feel it immensely. Sir Neville informed us that you and Mr. Smithson found him." Gregson shook his head. "I do not envy you. Such a sight must surely produce the most gruesome nightmares."

"We shall see, of course. I haven't had to put my dreams to the test yet. Did you know the baron well?"

"Not more than one does meeting frequently in society, you know. And we saw him last summer at Ranleigh, of course, but he only stayed a short while. I suppose he had other pressing engagements. Mrs. Gregson was related to the late baroness, but Tunwell was not one to discuss family matters, so I do not think we ever actually spoke on the subject."

"London is such a large place that I can see how one might spend one's whole life attending parties and so forth and never actually speak of anything important to another person."

Mr. Gregson did not seem to appreciate Althea's attempt at wit. He turned a rather dour face to her. "I understand from our good host that you spend most of your time in Somerset and were in London for only part of last season."

"Yes. The untimely death of our cousin put a stop to all of our London revels. After his demise, it did not seem fair to burden the Marquess of Levanwood and his good lady with our presence any longer. We therefore accepted the invitation and stayed some weeks with our friend, Lady Bertlesmon, at Norwich House. We returned to Dettamoor Park before the season was out."

"I am sorry for the loss of your cousin. His tragic death at the hands of those marauders shook all of us to the core. No one is safe upon the streets of London!"

Althea, who used to play on her widow bereavement in order to discourage unwanted suitors, assumed a pious expression suitable for a bereaved cousin and said, "Thank you, sir. We feel his loss tremendously. This is why I can so empathize with the late baron's family. Mr. Cruikshank has my deepest sympathies."

"And mine too, I am sure. Not that a fellow of Cruikshank's reputation is likely to feel as he ought at his uncle's passing."

"I have heard that he is quite wild."

"Unpardonably wild. It is a wonder Lord Tunwell continued to support him as he did."

"Family is family, after all."

"True, but supporting a wastrel only allows him to continue in vice," Mr. Gregson said sternly.

Althea had the sense that Mr. Gregson was one of those skinflint persons unlikely to support anyone, however virtuous, and said, "I hear that Mr. Cruikshank will soon be with us. I will admit that I am a little curious to meet such depravity in person. I have lived such a sheltered life up to now that I have never actually met a wastrel. My neighbors in Somerset are all very respectable, and if I can be so bold, somewhat dull in their habits."

Mr. Gregson responded as if humoring a child. "To be sure. I see that the general opinion is quite correct in attributing to your ladyship a wry wit."

Althea bit back a retort that was considerably sharper than the term *wry* would imply, but then thought better of antagonizing a gentleman who was obviously much stricter in his opinions on propriety than Althea. She returned a rather thin smile. "Indeed, my opinions are often not my own."

After supper, the ladies retired for tea and coffee and insipid conversation. Jane had the good fortune to strike up a conversation with Lady Pickney, and so Althea was left with Mrs. Gregson, who seemed very much the average London matron with little in her head but fashion and gossip. Mrs. Gregson, curious about Althea's sudden social prominence, peppered her with pointed questions. She clearly desired to elicit any information that could adequately explain how a country nobody could have become the much talked of Lady Trent. And, assuming this prominence was due entirely to the Duke of Norwich, what a man of his stamp could have seen in a drab widow from Somerset.

Althea wondered whether any of this was adequately explained by the time the men joined the party, but was too happy to escape the conversation to wait for the answer. She entered very willingly in a game of whist with Sir Neville, Lord Pickney, and Jane, and spent the rest of the evening quite pleasantly.

She went up the stairs to bed, but instead of getting under the covers, plead sleeplessness and sent Miss Dorkins to her bed between the rooms. Fortunately for Althea's plans, Miss Dorkins was hard to rouse under any circumstances, and so certainly wouldn't wake at the cat-like steps of Althea. Althea desired to sneak downstairs unobserved in order to return the fob to the body before Mr. Cruikshank or anyone else noticed that it had gone missing. Plus, she wanted another look at the corpse.

Althea's father, Dr. William Claire, being a renowned physician, had seen death in many forms. Althea, frequently taken along to act as his nurse and helper, was also privileged to acquire a profound understanding of the myriad ways human life could be ended. It was an unfortunate thing that dissection was so difficult to practice outside of certain learned schools of medicine, because Althea knew how much could be discovered about a disease state through a careful examination of a body, inside and out. However, barring that, even a superficial examination could yield otherwise hidden answers.

After a suitable wait for the rest of the house to retire, Althea pulled her wrapper tight. *Carpe noctem*, she thought, and carefully opened the door. She covered the candle flame with her hand, protecting it from the droughts of the hallway, and preventing too much light from seeping under the doors of her fellow house guests. She made her way to the old wing without mishap and, once in that part of the house, held the candle high as she traversed a back hallway that no guest had been required to use because Sir Neville, the Gregsons, and the Pickneys had rooms closer to the newer end of the house.

She found the body much as Miss Dorkins had described it, laid out on an old table set in the middle of the room with a sheet drawn over the corpse. Althea removed the sheet from the top half of the body. The body had not shown signs of *rigor mortis* when pulled from the pond and so was able to be placed face up flat upon the table's surface, with the arms crossed over the chest as if in repose. Enough time had passed, however, that the limbs were stiff in place. Several blankets had been placed under the corpse and those were damp, while the clothes were relatively dry.

Someone had taken the trouble to clean Lord Tunwell's face and close his eyes, but the clothing was still muddy and pieces of plant matter clung to it. There was a distinct odor of pond mud and plants layered over with the smell of early putrefaction. While others might have recoiled, the smells reminded Althea of her father, and a wave of nostalgia washed over her. How often she wished he were still alive. But, never mind the useless daydreaming, she must get to work before someone found her.

Althea carefully slipped the fob back into the pocket where the watch now reposed and then set about to examine the body for any anomalies that might argue against death as a result of a slip and fall into the pond. The head appeared to be intact, and as she traced her fingers along the skull, she could feel no indentations or other indicators of a blow to the head, unless the blow had been aimed at the base of the skull where she could not reach.

The mouth was partially open and so she held her candle aloft and peered in between the jaws. There was mud and bracken in the teeth, which might indicate an intake of breath while in the water. There also appeared to be some blood. Althea held the candle closer, careful not to drip wax on the corpse. The tongue was the likely culprit for the blood, as the surface appeared to be lacerated. The baron must have bit down upon it as he went into the water.

As she moved down the body, she could discern nothing else that would argue against a slip and fall. As she had noted by the pond, the sleeves of Lord Tunwell's jacket were ripped and his hands scratched, as if he had struggled against the reeds to pull himself out. The fingernails were jagged. Althea looked more closely. Lord Tunwell's nails exhibited horizontal stripes of white. She changed the angle of the candle, thinking that perhaps the stripes were ridges instead. No, the nails were definitely striped. That certainly didn't fit with everything she had heard so far.

After examining the top half of the body, Althea replaced the sheet and then focused on the legs and feet. The baron was dressed in the buckskin breeches and boots common in the country, but his boots were clearly of no recent date. In fact, the heels of both feet were quite worn. Such a pair of boots could explain a slip on a muddy bank. The worn leather would not have provided any traction.

Taken together, the examination had produced nothing that would argue against an accidental death, so Althea placed the sheet as she had found it and retraced her steps back to her room. She peeked into the antechamber and heard the sonorous breathing of Miss Dorkins. She closed the door and then climbed into bed. She fell asleep still puzzling over it all.

CHAPTER SEVEN

The next morning dawned bright, and Althea got up early for a walk around the rose garden before she breakfasted. The roses seemed even lovelier in the morning light with the dew still on their silken petals. She was just watching the lazy flight of a fat bumble bee when she heard a rustle behind her. She turned and met the sheepish stare of a young gardener, basket in hand.

"Sorry to disturb you, ma'am, but Sir Neville has ordered fresh flowers for the house."

"Then I am the one disturbing you. Please pay me no mind. Sir Neville has such a lovely garden that I couldn't help but come out here to enjoy the morning in it."

"It is indeed mighty fine," he replied.

"Have you been at Ranleigh a long time Mr. —"

"Ogden. They call me Ogden, ma'am." He blushed furiously and looked down.

Althea smiled encouragingly. "A long time, Mr. Ogden?"

"All my life, ma'am. My family has always served the Tabards."

"I see. Then you are the perfect person to tell me everything I want to know about the ornamental pond."

"Yes ma'am, I helped dig it out."

The next half hour passed very pleasantly as Althea received all sorts of interesting information about the construction of the pond, the planting of reeds and other aquatic specimens, and the stocking of it with fish in case some guest of the Tabard family was inclined to be an angler. In between this conversation, Althea and Ogden discussed which roses to cut and how to cut them so as not to damage the plant.

Finally, Althea felt that she had detained Ogden enough for one morning and returned back to the house and her breakfast. Jane had come down and was seated beside Lady Pickney, who was just tucking into a large steak.

"I had wondered where you got to," Jane said. "Did you have a nice walk?"

Althea turned to Lady Pickney, "Miss Trent knows my habits well enough by now to know that I must have some activity as soon as I am up. Today, I had the pleasure of wandering through the rose garden. It is simply delightful."

Lady Pickney nodded. "I have no doubt. I will have to get Lord Pickney to take me around the estate. Or perhaps we can convince our host to organize a tour in his curricle, as I am no great walker."

Althea selected some eggs and a piece of toast from the sideboard and then sat down opposite Jane. "I'm sure such a scheme could be arranged, although perhaps it is too soon for merriment. When does Mr. Cruikshank arrive?"

"I am told he comes this afternoon. Lord and Lady Batterslea were also to arrive today, but heaven knows if they will come now. Miss Trent, do you know?"

Jane refused to be trapped. "I am not in Sir Neville's confidence, and so I could not tell you."

"Well, if they cry off because poor Lord Tunwell had an accident, it will be too bad. However, I do hope Mr. Cruikshank won't be staying more than is necessary. His presence in this house cannot be considered a beneficial one," Lady Pickney said.

Althea smiled. "But surely Miss Trent and I are above temptation of that sort, and clearly your ladyship cannot be in any danger of succumbing to the charms of a rake, however handsome."

Lady Pickney returned the smile. "No indeed. It is merely I fear some unpleasant behavior on Mr. Cruikshank's part, for who knows what tricks a man like that may get up to holed up in the country with a sedate group of visitors?"

"Indeed," Althea replied, "who knows?" But she was more curious than ever to make Mr. Cruikshank's acquaintance.

Later that afternoon, Althea's curiosity was satisfied when a dashing phaeton rolled into the curling drive of Ranleigh, pulled by a pair of high-stepping gray horses. Mr. Cruikshank descended with a flourish, his many-caped greatcoat flying behind him. He doffed his high crowned beaver hat to the Dettamoor Park ladies, who stood in solidarity with Sir Neville in his time of trial in front of the house. Jane looked at Althea with raised eyebrows, but Althea made no answering remark. Her eyes could not be moved from the face of the most beautiful man she had ever beheld.

It was as if she were staring at the face of an angel painted on the ceiling of a church. His skin was porcelain fair and he had long golden curls, faintly tinged with red, that hung around his face. His eyes were a clear blue, Althea noticed, and his mouth was so well-formed that Althea had to force her eyes away from it. *I can see now why Mr. Cruikshank is so dangerous*, she thought. *Too bad the face of an angel conceals the heart of a devil.*

"So, I finally meet the famous Lady Trent," Cruikshank said, with a saucy smile.

Althea, who was no simpering miss, replied calmly, "Unfortunately, the circumstances are none too pleasant, sir. You have my deepest sympathies," and then after a pause, "I trust your journey was not too difficult?"

"The fatigues of the journey are amply rewarded by the sight of your ladyship. You know, you are quite as pretty as they say, Lady Trent."

Althea refused to be baited. "I am unaware of the rumors, so I don't know how to give that a proper reply. I will, however, take that as a compliment, if it was meant as one."

Cruikshank's smile grew broader. "Oh it was, Lady Trent."

"Then do please join us inside for some refreshment."

"Yes, yes," Sir Neville added. "You are very welcome at Ranleigh."

Mr. Cruikshank's reception by the other members of the party was quite chilly, however. He received the faintest of bows from the Gregsons and cold nods from Lord and Lady Pickney. Mr. Smithson merely extended him a bored greeting. Silence then reigned in the rose drawing room. Althea busied herself with pouring Mr. Cruikshank a cup of tea and handed it to him, saying, "Should you desire some cake, Lord Tunwell?"

"Why, yes." Cruikshank surveyed the room with an air of benevolence. "I believe you are the first person to address me by my new title, Lady Trent. I must say it sounds very well, don't you think?"

"I am sure you will grow accustomed to it," she replied. "One slice of cake or two?"

"Certainly two. One cannot stop to eat when one is racing to retrieve one's deceased uncle."

Sir Neville, trying, for the sake of propriety, to say something before Cruikshank could continue this inappropriate line of conversation, made a remark on the weather. Jane joined in, and between the two of them, filled the room with bubbly chatter about the weather and the prospect of pulling together a riding party to Summit Hill, a local landmark. Althea encouraged them with bits of her own observations on the rose garden and other pleasures of Ranleigh. Slowly but surely, the others joined in, until Cruikshank seemed to be quite forgotten.

Mr. Cruikshank watched them all over the rim of his teacup with a faint curl of the lip and an expression of boredom for twenty minutes or so. Then, perhaps perceiving that there was no end to Sir Neville's conversation, got up and said, "I suppose it can't be helped. Take me to the body. If the present company will spare me, I must pay my respects to my dear uncle."

There was a gasp from Mrs. Gregson and a suppressed giggle from Lady Pickney. Sir Neville bounded out of his chair, his corset creaking so loudly that Althea thought the whalebones would surely break, to politely hustle the unwanted visitor out of the room.

When the extraction of Mr. Cruikshank was complete, Mr. Gregson said, "What an impudent young puppy! I have no patience with the man."

"Did you see the color of his waistcoat? I would never have dared to wear pink with a green coat. It is positively monstrous," said Mr. Smithson, with a pained expression.

Lady Pickney's giggle turned into a full throated laugh. "I will give him his due, he does know how to liven up this party."

"Really, my dear," said her husband, "I don't know that the house party needed Mr. Cruikshank's appearance for that."

"Still, one must make allowances for Mr. Cruikshank. He has suffered the loss of his uncle," said Althea.

"Best thing that could have happened to the man. Otherwise, he'd be clapped in irons in a debtor's prison," said Mr. Gregson.

"I'm sure it can't be as bad as that," said Jane.

"It very likely is," Lady Pickney said. "The baron's death is quite timely. Still, it will not be easy to get the body buried at Tunwell Court. It is practically in Scotland."

Sometime later, Althea, who had taken the opportunity to explore the grounds of Ranleigh once again and was just coming back to the front of the house, saw several men hoisting an unwieldy coffin covered with black fabric into a large farm cart. They were supervised by Mr. Cruikshank and Sir Neville. Once that was accomplished, two of the men climbed up and took the reins. When the cart had lumbered up the drive, Althea approached Cruikshank and Sir Neville. She noticed that Mr. Cruikshank's green coat was now adorned with a black armband.

"Lady Trent," Sir Neville said, "we have now completed this sad business. I have begged Mr. Cruikshank to stay another evening before he makes his way to Tunwell Court for the funeral services. One cannot travel so much in one day. It is too fatiguing on the body."

"Indeed, I think that is wise," Althea said.

"Have you been walking the grounds?" Mr. Cruikshank asked.

Althea nodded. "I am accounted a great walker and cannot stand to be cooped up in a small room on such a fine day."

"Then let me take a turn with you. Sir Neville was just telling me that there are some fine walks beyond the pond. But then, perhaps you do not wish to visit the pond. I have been told that you were the enterprising person who found my late uncle."

"I am not injured by the experience, I assure you."

When they were out of earshot of Sir Neville, Althea said, "Let me take this moment to express my condolences once again. The death of one's uncle in such a fashion must be terribly distressing."

"Inconvenient, certainly, but not distressing. I think I shall like being Lord Tunwell much better than I liked being Mr. Cruikshank. Besides, my uncle and I never got along. He was too stiff and I was too rebellious."

"And do you feel that having the benefits of the title shall curb some of the rebellion?"

"Undoubtedly. I am feeling stiffer by the minute."

Althea chuckled. "I would take care, Lord Tunwell, that you do not use your new position to simply augment your prior habits. Money may do a great deal of harm with the wrong object."

"Duly noted, Lady Trent. But what do you know of poverty and want? Surely you have never been kept like a puppet on a string by a stingy skinflint of an uncle."

"No, my husband was kind and generous with me. But I did not grow up as the wife of a baronet. My father was eminently respectable, but we never lived in the style most inhabitants of London would think indispensable for happiness."

"You intrigue me greatly, Lady Trent. What sort of life was that?"

"My father was a noted physician, sir, and dedicated his too short life to the curing of the sick and the pursuit of knowledge. Given that you now have the means, I would urge you to dedicate your life to some useful purpose."

Mr. Cruikshank threw back his head and laughed. "So you urge me to become an honest man, do you? Unfortunately, I do not think you can turn a sinner into a saint in the space of a day, even with such an eloquent reproof. I have always done just what I shouldn't, and if I am to be honest, I don't see that money or a title can make much of a difference."

"That is, of course, up to your own conscience. I merely suggest that you consider carefully before you return to London and your prior life."

"Well, that at least I can promise. The funeral shall require me to rusticate at Tunwell Court for at least a fortnight."

"Perhaps the country life will suit you."

"It hasn't yet. Every visit to Tunwell Court was an exercise in excruciating boredom. Country hours, deplorable food, and inferior company do not suit me now, and I don't think they ever will."

"I find the country quite delightful. And although the company may be restricted, I think that the fresh air, beautiful scenery, and healthful exercise more than make up for any defects. Besides, you have only to take on your own chef to rectify the food, invite your particular friends for company, and set your hours as you please. As long as your income will allow for a sufficient candle budget, that is."

"Eminently practical advice, Lady Trent. Perhaps I shall take it." They were at the pond by this time and Mr. Cruikshank pointed to the bank. "So this is where the old fellow fell in, is it?"

Althea nodded. "Just there, beyond that bend, by the bulrushes. I am not sure what made him approach so close to the water, but the bank is very slippery just there. He apparently slid in and was unable to extricate himself from the rushes. I assume that he did not know how to swim."

Mr. Cruikshank turned to her, a slight frown on his perfect brow. "That is a little strange, for he had spent some time in the East Indies in his youth, and I particularly remember him telling me once of swimming in a river full of silver fish. But that was many years ago, when he was still a young man. No doubt he had lost his skill with the passage of time." Mr. Cruikshank suddenly smiled. "Or he actually had the apoplexy I had wished for all those years." He looked at Althea, perhaps to see if his remark had shocked her, but he underestimated his audience.

"That would account for it, certainly. Did your uncle have a bad heart?"

"I think I've mentioned that he had no heart."

"I take that answer to mean that you were not in his confidence with regard to his state of health?"

"No, I was not. I must say, Lady Trent, you have a very singular manner. I can see now what Norwich finds so alluring. Nothing I say perturbs you in the least."

"I think we have strayed into the one topic that will. Shall we take a turn around the pond?"

"Ah, so the gossip is correct. I have twenty guineas riding on Norwich coming up to scratch at the moment, so any information you could give me on the subject would be much appreciated."

Althea took a deep breath, controlling her features into the mask of civility she put on with people she found impertinent. "I would not hazard a guess, I am afraid. You perhaps should ask His Grace about his future plans."

Cruikshank's angel face broke out in devilish smile. He grabbed Althea's hand before she could protest and brought it to his lips. "Perhaps I should cancel the bet and make a go of it myself. I could get used to a wife."

CHAPTER EIGHT

And then, as if by magic, he was in the water with a giant splash and a great flapping of arms. Althea turned and saw the source of this magic, a very angry Duke of Norwich.

"My lord!" she gasped, but Norwich was still addressing the soggy Cruikshank.

"And if I ever catch you so much as looking the wrong way at Lady Trent, you shall have me to answer to!"

"My lord, I don't know that he can swim. We must not let him drown like his uncle."

"I don't care."

"Do be sensible." She looked around for something to fish Cruikshank out, and seeing a large stick laying in the grass, retrieved it. "Lord Tunwell, just grab on to the end and we will pull you out."

Norwich grimly took the stick from her and extended it out into the pond. Cruikshank got hold of it and emerged from the pond a muddy, sopping mess. He seemed in good humor, however, and winked at Althea when Norwich couldn't see. "I believe I have won my bet, after all."

When he was some distance away, walking leisurely and whistling a jaunty tune, Althea turned on Norwich, "Just what are you doing here?"

"Defending your honor against the likes of the new baron. Did you want that impudent rascal to paw you like the animal he is?"

"No, of course not, but I think you know me well enough to know that I can handle myself. Now you have given him the very information that I was seeking to hide."

"I make no apologies. You should not have been out walking alone with the likes of that fellow. You can have no idea what a man like that is capable of."

"As you well know, my dealings with my late cousin have given me ample experience with evil disguised as respectability. At least Lord Tunwell makes no secret of his conduct. Besides, I was attempting to get him to see the error of his ways."

"The error of his ways? Only you would think to lecture a lecherous reprobate." Then Norwich stopped and laughed. "Oh Althea, I have missed you." He held out his hand. "Come, my love, and cry peace."

Althea realized for the thousandth time why he had been the most sought-after bachelor in London. There was something in the charm of his manner and the sparkle in his eye that set her heart to flutter in a most undignified manner. She looked around and, seeing that Cruikshank was some distance, put her hand in his. "We must be careful of prying eyes, my lord. I was not expecting you."

Norwich looked at Cruikshank's retreating figure. "I can see not."

"But how have you left your mother and your other engagements in Bath?"

"Hang Bath. My mother will survive without me. I came straight away once I got your letter. I think you are in some danger, and it would be best if you and Jane retired to Dettamoor Park as soon as possible."

"No, Sir Neville would never forgive us. Besides, I don't see that the demise of the baron portends ill for us."

"I had a visit from my brother last week and, given our previous confidence, he saw fit to inform me, among other disclosures, that the deceased Lord Tunwell was under heightened suspicion by the government. He thought I might hear something of some use. Little did I think you would be involved!"

"You should thank God I was involved, for I have something I wish to show you. Let us walk back to the house."

Norwich extended his arm and Althea took it, conscious of how near to her he was. She could smell the faint whiff of his usual cologne and the fragrance muddled her thoughts in a way she couldn't quite explain.

"I was the one who found the body. Well, Mr. Smithson and I, but he was too frightened to enter the water and retrieve it," Althea said, to bring her mind back into a better course.

Norwich turned to her. "Let me anticipate the next part of the story. You entered the water to pull the body out."

"Yes, of course." Then she laughed. "You should have seen my abigail's face when she saw what a mess I'd made of my blue muslin dress."

"I can only imagine. But the obvious question is, why did you think you could pull a man the size of Lord Tunwell out of the pond?"

"I'll admit I wasn't thinking rationally."

"A rare admission."

"You are too severe with me, my lord."

He stopped and looked down into her face. "Robert. Please, Althea, I would like to hear my name on your lips just once."

"Very well. You are too severe with me, Robert."

"Lovely. Now we may continue with this engaging story." They started walking again. "You tried to pull the baron out of the pond, but only succeeded in ruining your dress."

"Yes, but as I did, I pulled a watch fob off of his watch chain and inside the fob I later found a piece of paper that I think you should see. When we get to the house, do you think you can make your way to my room? I am in the fourth room on the right of the new wing."

"Why, my love, is that an invitation?"

"Not that kind of invitation, Your Grace. The paper is in the back of my wardrobe, and I don't wish us to be seen."

"If you stop saying *Your Grace* I will refrain from teasing you."

"A fair trade. Can you meet me there?"

"That should be quite easy. Sir Neville has kindly placed me in the fifth room on the right."

They separated before approaching the house, and Althea, who knew the house quite well by this point, found the back stairs. She made it to her room without being seen, and then had the presence of mind to lock the door between her room and Miss Dorkin's ante chamber. When Norwich rapped quietly, she was already at the hall door, ready to open it.

She closed the door behind him and latched it. "Please be seated. It will take me just a moment to dig it out."

He did as she requested, but she felt his eyes on her as she went to the wardrobe. "Here it is," she said after a moment. "Let me just untie the ribbon. I slipped it in between your letters."

"So you keep my letters?"

"Yes, of course. I keep all of my correspondence. This is it." She handed him the slip of paper and then sat down in the opposite chair. "What do you make of that?"

He held it up to the light of the window and turned it over. "*Al Andalus.*"

"The Moorish name for Spain. I fear it may have something to do with the peninsular campaign."

"It could. Or it could have another meaning, perhaps some sort of code. What are these lines?"

"I don't know, but they could be a map. What did your brother tell you about the baron?"

"Nothing more than that he was under suspicion. Lord Tunwell was a friend to several men of high position in the cabinet and so could have had access to important information, if he turned thief."

"But why would Lord Tunwell desire to do such a thing? He had no need of money for himself, and he certainly wasn't spending more than necessary on his nephew, because from what I have heard, that gentleman was just this side of debtors' prison."

"You would do well to stay away from Cruikshank."

"Be that as it may, have you found fault with my logic?"

"Not yet. I will send word express to George and see what he thinks. Sir Neville told me that Lord Tunwell slipped into the pond and drowned. You saw the body in the pond. Does that explanation hold? It sounded from your letter that it did not."

"It could have happened that way, but the water was up to the level of my chest and the baron was a large, tall man. I find it hard to believe that such a man could drown on his own without a blow to the head or something to render him unconscious. Unfortunately, I could find no evidence of anything unusual on the back of his skull. Mind you, if the blow was down where the head joins the neck, I might not have felt it. *Rigor mortis* had set in so I couldn't move the head to check."

Norwich's face went a shade whiter and then flushed red. "I might have known. You examined the corpse, didn't you?"

"Yes, but it was only a cursory examination. I didn't disrobe him or perform an anatomical study."

"And what if someone had caught you?"

"It was late at night so no one saw me. Besides, I had to return the fob before someone missed it."

Norwich looked at her sternly and then sighed, seemingly resigned. "Let me take charge of the paper. I do not wish you to court such danger again." Norwich pulled a large gold pocket watch out of his vest pocket and then pressed down on the edge of the case. The back of the watch opened and he placed the paper there and closed the back up. "I will let you know when I hear from my brother. In the meantime, do not say anything of this to anyone, not even Jane."

"I haven't spoken to Jane. I did not wish to concern her when she needs to be focused on determining if she is to be Lady Tabard."

"And you? Have you decided to be a Duchess?"

"I told you that I need six months."

"I have never met two women so unwilling to experience the joys of matrimony."

"Come now, let us be honest with each other. You would not be half so eager were I one of those simpering young misses whose mothers have thrown them in your way for the last decade. With that sort of fate awaiting you, it's a wonder that you have any taste for matrimony at all."

Norwich gave her a warm look. "I know what awaits me."

Althea knew that she was in dangerous waters, and so replied matter-of-factly, "A duke must have an heir, after all."

"The heir is of secondary importance. Do not play coy. I know that women have the same desires as men."

"Your superior knowledge must defeat any argument of mine, but give me your hand, if you please."

He extended his large hand and she took it in both of hers, examining the fingernails closely. "Very good. I might still be prevailed upon to marry you."

"What does that mean?"

"Your nails do not have white lines on them."

"And if they did?"

"Did you know the baron when he was young?"

"He was my elder by at least ten years. When he was young, I was not yet breeched."

"So you wouldn't have heard any rumors of debauchery, not even when you first went upon the town?"

"Here, Althea, I promise you that my past is past. My days of debauchery, if any really existed, need not trouble you."

"Not you, Lord Tunwell."

"The man lived like a monk for all of my acquaintance with him. What has any of this to do with anything?"

"Then perhaps it was a mere fling. In any case, I can hardly picture it."

"For the love of all that is holy, would you tell me what you are getting at?"

"His fingernails showed the white stripes typical of someone who has taken arsenic over a long period of time and, unless the arsenic was accidentally ingested, which I doubt, he was likely prescribed it for the treatment of the French pox. Or syphilis, as doctors call it. My father had several patients with much the same condition and, in my opinion, arsenic is the only treatment that has a chance of being effective. Mercury is the more popular one, but tends to have deleterious effects on the mind. *Aegrescit medendo.*"

"It's a wonder you have any delicacy of mind the way your father took you about."

She let go of his hand. "I have very little, as you well know. In any case, it is a useful fact. A woman must be careful."

"It could happen to anyone."

"I know that, but debauchery does increase the odds. In any case, it is an unimportant detail, but something that seemed out of character for such a solid citizen. Then again, if Lord Tunwell was also spying for the French, it just shows how little one knows of one's fellow men."

"Sometimes," Norwich replied, a crease between his brows.

There was a moment of uncomfortable silence until Althea said, "I think that you may safely return to your room now."

Norwich stood and Althea followed, but he didn't turn towards the door. Instead, he reached his hand out and gently traced the contours of her face. His touch was soft and yet somehow electric. She looked up and his eyes held hers, pulling her to him. And then he was nearer than he had been before, so near that she caught the smell of his cologne mingled with the starch of his shirt. She lowered her eyes and her gaze landed on the soft fullness of his lips. It was the strangest thing, her sudden desire to feel those lips on hers. She tried to rationally analyze the situation, but her brain did not respond the way it ought.

"You can't deny this," he said.

"But I should try," she replied. "You must go now, sir. If anyone caught us, my reputation would not stand the assault."

"Robert. And we would only have to formally announce our engagement to make it right."

He leaned down as if to kiss her, but she stepped back. "Robert. You know your mother would never consent to our marriage under those circumstances."

"My mother has no say in the matter." Despite these brave words, he disengaged himself and straightened his cravat. "However, I see that militant look in your eye, and frankly, I don't know if I can trust myself under the circumstances."

He looked quickly at the four poster bed and then back at her.

"How long are you staying?" she said, still shaken.

"Trying to send me away?"

"No, it's just that I find I can't think properly with you here at Ranleigh."

"All the better. I am here for as long as it takes to unravel this issue with the baron, and for my mother to travel with my sister back to Austell Abbey, thus alleviating my obligations in Bath."

"Oh."

Norwich took her hand and kissed it. "I promise it won't be too terrible."

CHAPTER NINE

Althea managed to avoid Norwich for the rest of the day. She still felt unsettled about how difficult it seemed to resist him. It wasn't like her to succumb to passion. She needed time to know what was right for her and her young son. And yet when she thought of telling him *no*, it made her feel inexplicably lonely.

When she and Jane descended for dinner, they realized that Lord and Lady Batterslea had arrived in the afternoon. He was a plain man, approaching middle age, who had lately come into the title upon the death of his ancient father. He was known to be extremely wealthy and well connected. His wife was one of those schoolroom misses Althea had described to the duke, who had successfully landed Lord Batterslea within her first season due to her renowned beauty. In close proximity, her beauty was even more radiant than glimpsed from across a crowded ballroom. Althea immediately felt the force of all of her own brown-haired drabness.

Althea and Jane were again consigned to the nether regions of the table with the Gregsons and Mr. Smithson, much to the obvious consternation of Norwich, who quickly surmised that the seating arrangement would give the new baron ample opportunity to make up to Althea, seated just below him. Norwich shot her a look of warning that Cruikshank perceived, as well. Cruikshank took full advantage of the situation, saying to Althea, "I think your protector is none too pleased with me, but rank must be observed, must it not?"

"It usually is. May I ask an impertinent question?"

"Those are the best kind."

"Why do you delight in shocking society?"

"I had heard you described as a lady with a frank and open manner, but I now see that the reports fell short of the mark. Do I shock society?" Cruikshank said.

"We never chanced to meet at Almack's, and so I assume that your reputation must have done you in with the patronesses, as you are clearly a man of birth and breeding."

"If admittance to Almack's is a sign of respectability, then I prefer to be a rake. It is far more agreeable."

"I suppose in a certain light it is, but do you not wish for some measure of acceptance from your fellow creatures?" Althea said.

"I wish to do exactly as I please when I please. If others do not find that acceptable, that is their problem. I am sure that is why my dear uncle was always threatening to cut me off."

"You may think differently once you have a wife and family."

He gave her a look that appeared to Althea's untrained eye at an attempt at seduction. "I am entranced with the picture you paint of domestic felicity, but I have not, as yet, met the woman who could tempt me."

Althea ignored the implication. "I am sure one day that you shall, and then you may see if I am not correct. Life is never what one expects. For the good or for the bad. Your uncle's death was most untimely, and it is a lesson to us all to do what we are meant to do before it is too late." And then she smiled inwardly to hear herself parroting the duke's words to her. *Perhaps Cruikshank and I are more similar than we seem.*

"Which just proves why I should not be bound by the strictures of society. Life is too short to suffer such non-sense. If I was willing to risk my inheritance before, I am not likely to change my mind now."

"But there is comfort and peace in routine. I am sure your uncle came to understand this as he grew older. Or perhaps he was always of a staid disposition?"

"As long as I knew him. Then again, he was much older than me."

Althea was about to reply when she heard the trill of high-pitched laughter. She glanced down towards the end of the table where Norwich was apparently making himself very agreeable to the beautiful Lady Batterslea. Althea found herself unaccountably gritting her teeth. *No matter,* she told herself, turning resolutely to the new baron. "I've been told that his marriage was a happy one, a love match, in fact."

"I believe it was. Although my aunt Livia died when I was young, so I never formed much of an opinion about her. My mother told me once that Livia had a touch of madness and that that was the reason she and the baron lived so retired before her death, but I remember nothing out of the ordinary. Then again, if I had to live with a man as stiff and boring as the baron, I'm sure I would go mad myself."

The voice of Lady Batterslea carried over the table, "Your Grace is too droll!"

Cruikshank's mouth twitched. "Norwich certainly knows how to bring home the point with you. He is accounted such a great matrimonial prize that I wonder at your hesitation."

Althea refused to dignify that remark with an answer. Instead she said, "And so you leave us tomorrow morning?"

"Yes, but Sir Neville has been kind enough to offer his home to me should I desire respite from the labor of my uncle's funeral ceremonies."

"And will you take him up on that generous offer?"

He gave Althea a saucy look. "I might be induced to do so."

Althea gave him back a quelling stare, which only served to produce a brilliant smile, transforming his face once again into that of an angel. "Yes," he added, "the temptation may be too great to resist."

After dinner, the ladies retired and Althea found herself sitting beside Lady Batterslea.

"And how do you find Ranleigh, Lady Batterslea? Is it not delightful?"

Lady Batterslea sipped her tea with the air of one who desires to appear sophisticated, but is not sure how to go about it. She feigned a bored air and said, "It is much the same as it was last summer.

"You have been here often?"

"We were here a year ago, after my marriage to Lord Batterslea. You were not in London last season, I understand."

"No, my home is in Somerset."

"That explains it, then. We made quite a merry party last summer."

Her dig wasn't lost on Althea, who gave her a wan smile. "Well, I find Ranleigh as beautiful as I was led to expect. The rose garden alone was worth the journey, but I hear that Sir Neville has kindly organized several excursions, including one even to the sea, which I must own would be beyond delightful."

Lady Batterslea looked down her nose. "The sea is tolerable when the sky is fair and there is little wind. One good breeze and the sand blows in one's face something terrible, beside the damage strong sun can do to a good complexion."

Althea, who had run out of civil remarks, sipped her tea quietly, hoping against hope that Jane, who was deep in conversation with Mrs. Gregson, would come rescue her, or that the men might be induced to cut their conversation short.

The latter occurred before the former, and as the men streamed in, Althea sought to catch Norwich's eye. He approached her, but, perhaps fearing being drawn into conversation with Lady Batterslea, remained just outside of the range of conversation. Instead, Lord Batterslea sat down beside them. He had the appearance of a man who is perfectly content with the privileges of his elevated station in life. He addressed Althea with an air of condolence, "I hear you had the misfortune to find Lord Tunwell, Lady Trent."

"Yes, Mr. Smithson and I found him."

"It is most distressing that you should be subjected to such horrors. One would not have had this happen for the world."

Althea wondered how Lord Batterslea would have prevented Tunwell's death, but said, "It was very sad, but I am on the path to recovering my composure, I assure you. He appears to have fallen in and been unable to climb back out. I am of the impression that he must not have been able to swim."

"Yes, I apprehend that that was the case. I only knew him socially, of course, but we had the privilege to pass some time together last summer here at Ranleigh."

"So Lady Batterslea was just telling me."

"I understand his nephew was not present when the sad death occurred."

"No," replied Althea, "he was sent for after the accident."

Batterslea smiled and then leaned in, "Good thing for him that he was, otherwise there might be talk."

"Surely no one would suspect the former Mr. Cruikshank of killing his uncle," Althea replied.

"Not openly, no, but Lord Tunwell could not have died too soon for the interest of his nephew. So, as you can see, his being in London at the time saves him from some awkward questions."

"Yes, I suppose so. Then again, the baron's death appears to have been an accidental drowning, so he couldn't have been implicated anyway."

"Is that what the apothecary determined?"

"I assume so. I was not present when he was called or when he examined the body."

"No, of course not, a gentle lady such as yourself wouldn't be. I am sorry, Lady Trent, for this line of most improper questions, but I had been told that you were of a scientific bent and so assumed you would not take my impertinence amiss. It is such a strange series of events, and coming so soon upon our arrival, I will admit to no little curiosity."

"No need to apologize. I perfectly understand. I too have been muddling over the baron's death. If someone had only been there at the time, it might have been prevented."

Althea was then called away to join Jane at the whist table, and so she excused herself and left Batterslea to the questionable charms of his wife.

Norwich had kept his distance all evening. When Althea climbed the stairs to her chamber in Jane's company, Jane said, "Have you and Norwich had a falling out over the handsome new baron?"

"No, of course not. The duke is merely respecting my wishes as to the privacy of our engagement. We can't be seen to be too familiar."

"Be careful you do not ask for too much distance or he may desire to end the engagement altogether."

"As Sir Neville has ended his because you have kept him at arm's length?"

Jane smiled. "Impudent child! I will leave you to your business, but mark my word, Norwich is not the kind of man to be trifled with."

"I have only ever been honest with him, as well he knows."

Miss Dorkins assisted Althea out of her dinner dress and into her nightdress and wrapper, and then Althea sent her away so that she might have a moment of quiet reflection with the latest *Philosophical Transactions*. There was a very fine article about the movement of the heavenly bodies that had caught her attention enough for a second, more detailed, reading.

She had not advanced very far when she heard a faint tapping at her door. She rose with a candle and then went quietly across the room. "Who is it?" she whispered through the keyhole.

But instead of a response the door opened quickly and Norwich stepped inside the room. He was still dressed for the evening in his breeches and coat. Althea stepped backward, clutching her wrapper across her chest with her other hand, feeling suddenly very exposed. "My lord, this is most irregular."

He shut the door behind him. "We shall have to keep our voices down. Is your abigail with you?"

Althea indicated the door to the ante room. "I assume that she has now retired to bed. But what are you about coming to me at night like this?"

"Don't tell me you are going to be missish. I cannot have private speech with you when you hold me off in public."

"I am only trying to keep our engagement between us. I would not want it said that I was throwing myself at you."

"No, merely making up to Cruikshank."

"Just as you were making yourself agreeable to the ravishing Lady Batterslea?"

"It was polite conversation."

"So was mine, except that I did try to get more information about the late baron out of him."

"So your flirting had a purpose? How very noble."

Althea gave him a look. "You wished to have private speech with me, Your Grace?"

He smiled, the tension easing from around his eyes. "Robert. You look beautiful with your hair down like that. I would have told you as much at the masquerade ball when you wore it that way with your beetle costume, except that I couldn't be sure you wouldn't have taken it amiss."

"I'm not sure why a compliment to my hair would have been more objectionable than the very indecent proposition you actually did make."

"And what proposal was that?"

"To be your mistress. Or have you regretted your words so completely that you have forgotten them?"

He chuckled. "No, but you know I want you for my wife. Unless you'd rather start with a discreet arrangement first? I will admit that seeing you here clothed only in a night-dress does make me imagine the possibilities."

Althea's face flushed. "What did you wish to speak to me about?"

"George arrives late tomorrow afternoon."

"So soon?"

"Apparently, the death of the baron is of greater import to the government than I had thought. George did not give me the particulars, but he wants to speak with us when he arrives."

"Do you think he will arrive before the new Lord Tunwell leaves?"

"Unlikely, unless Cruikshank delays his journey. Why do you ask?"

"Lord Batterslea said several things to me this evening that made me wonder if Cruikshank might have had something to do with his uncle's death."

"But he was in London," Norwich said.

"That is what I had understood, but what if he appeared to come from London, but instead came here ahead and murdered his poor uncle?"

"Glad to see you are finally coming to see the kind of man he is. But why should my brother want to see him?"

"I don't know – Cruikshank might also be connected in some way with that piece of paper," Althea said.

"If Cruikshank were a spy, he would not likely be facing a debtor's prison."

"True."

"Come Althea, it may just as easily have been an accident as anything else. The paper we found may not be in any way connected. We would be wise to let George handle the matter."

"Yes, I suppose you are correct."

There was a long pause. Norwich looked at her and then, before she had time to react, leaned down and brushed his lips against hers, in the barest hint of a kiss. "Good night, my love."

He straightened up and walked quickly to the door, closing it silently behind him.

CHAPTER TEN

Althea awoke early, as was her custom, and, after Miss Dorkins helped her to dress, she made her way down the stairs, determined to walk the grounds a little before breakfast and explore the scene of Lord Tunwell's death in case any new theory might occur to her. At the entrance of the house, she encountered Cruikshank, preparing to get an early start on his journey.

"Good morning, Lady Trent. How lovely to have you as a farewell party. I fear the rest of the household has been desiring my absence ere long."

"Well, to be perfectly frank, I had no notion you were to leave at this hour and merely meant to take a stroll before breakfast, as was my wont while at Dettamoor Park. My nature inclines me to mornings, you see."

Cruikshank smiled. "Your honesty disarms my sarcasm. I hope that when I have settled this business of my uncle, I may return to Ranleigh to enjoy the delights of the estate."

"Sir Neville has given the invitation. I wish you well on your journey, and hope that the somber nature of your errand causes you to engage in further sober reflection." Althea extended her hand to him as a gesture that the conversation was at an end.

He took her hand and kissed it with more feeling than was seemly. "Oh, I'm sure it must, Lady Trent, I'm sure it must."

He just means to tease me, Althea said to herself, as she left the close garden paths around the house and headed off towards the pond. *And set Norwich's back up.*

In the light of the fine summer morning, she had trouble considering Cruikshank as anything more than a spoiled young man who enjoyed the shock his antics produced in the minds of the more upstanding members of society. He certainly didn't seem the type to drown his uncle, a task that would have required cunning and tremendous strength. It was clear from the amount of plant matter attached to his clothes that the late baron had struggled once he was in the water – whether that was because he couldn't swim or because of the active intervention of another person remained to be seen.

Once Althea reached the pond, she made her way to the location of the drowning. The rushes appeared broken and matted as before, but the watery mud of the marsh had filled in the spaces of the baron's last footsteps. She noted with approval that the Ranleigh pond had a wide variety of vegetation encompassing multiple species of bull rushes, grasses and aquatic lily pads. There were even banded horsetail stalks with their pale rings, a perfect environment for all manner of insects and other pond wildlife.

A faint chirp caught her ear and she bent down to see a small speckled green frog, like those she had studied in the pond of Dettamoor Park, perched on a horsetail stem. She had meant to do further study on the life cycle of these frogs, but her sojourn to London had cut her study short. She bent over to examine the frog at closer range, hoping perhaps to catch sight of a glossy accumulation of eggs that would give her further information about its life cycle and mating habits. Perhaps she should have brought her notes from Dettamoor for a point of comparison, just as Jane had suggested. An examination of the frog's life cycle would make an excellent, albeit dull, second manuscript for the Royal Society.

She moved the horsetail stems apart with her gloved hand. No eggs seemed present in the watery muck, but Althea did notice a small white object tangled in amongst the leaves. She removed her glove so as to avoid ruining yet more clothing with the pond mud and picked the object up. It appeared to be a comfit. Althea raised it to her nose. An almond-flavored comfit by the smell of it. Odd, but not determinative of anything in particular, except that some visitor to the pond was fond of almond comfits to cleanse the breath and clear the palate of distasteful favors. She was about to throw it back, but then thought better of it. It might prove to be a clue of some sort. She tucked it into her reticule, and then decided to continue her walk around the circumference of the pond.

When she returned to the house, the breakfast parlor was filled with animated chatter. Lady Pickney was holding forth with the latest town scandal. She had eager listeners in Mr. Smithson and Mrs. Gregson.

"And then Lady Plimpton was forced to acknowledge that she had been with Lord Haverford when she said she was on a trip to Scotland. It was most shocking, and poor Lord Plimpton is beside himself. It will end in divorce, but whether Haverford will marry her, one can only guess."

"It is a disgraceful business," Mrs. Gregson said. "Haverford is nothing but a wanton libertine, and Lady Plimpton is worse for falling into his clutches."

"Yes, I suppose," Lady Pickney said, "but so diverting. The only thing I regret about the summer is the sad lack of diverting stories. Barring the poor baron, nothing very exciting ever seems to happen in the summer. At least, nothing worth repeating when one returns to town."

Jane gave Althea a sharp look of inquiry.

"I have been on a brisk walk," Althea informed the group, breaking in upon Lady Pickney. "I find that it is very healthful for the digestion, and there are such lovely paths here at Ranleigh."

"So true," Mrs. Gregson replied, now seeming happy to change the subject. "I had not realized you were such a determined walker, Lady Trent. I too find walking to be delightful exercise. We must walk together some afternoon, if the sun is not too fierce."

"I should like that very much," Althea replied, serving herself some eggs from the chafing dish. "Of course, if anyone else desires to walk with us, we would be only too happy."

"Oh no, I will leave you two to your promenades. I fear my slow pace would only hold you back," Lady Pickney said.

"I find the summer sun exhausting," added Mr. Smithson in a languid voice.

"I had thought that perhaps we could take a tour of Ranleigh on horseback. There are some delightful woods and streams beyond the south pasture. That is, if the ladies would not find an easy canter over the countryside too strenuous," Sir Neville said.

There was general approval of the scheme, and after breakfast, Jane and Althea retired to their rooms to change into their riding habits. They met Miss Dorkins, who was full of energy at the prospect of assisting Jane and Althea into what she termed were the finest riding costumes she had ever laid eyes on.

"Sir Neville has assured me that he has just the horses for our tastes," Jane said, as Miss Dorkins fastened a deep green spencer jacket over her rose habit. Jane's spencer was trimmed with lace dyed to match the rose fabric of her habit, and the softness of the lace contrasted with Jane's naturally severe aspect. It made her seem younger, more like the girl who had first come into society. She topped the outfit with a fetching bonnet that framed her face.

"Tame, in other words," replied Althea. "I fear that my sad lack of horsemanship shall give a lie to my now elevated position. My, Jane, you are teasing poor Sir Neville with that outfit. He will fall more deeply in love than ever."

"I could say the same to you."

Althea's dress took the opposite tack to Jane's, emphasizing her fine features and small neat figure with a structured blue dress adorned with gold braiding, as if Althea were some Amazon commander queen. She topped it with a shako style bonnet that she rakishly wore at an angle.

The Dettamoor Park ladies descended the stairs to find that their party had been augmented by Mr. Gregson and Lord Pickney and the duke. There was an appreciative gleam in Norwich's eyes as his gaze met Althea's, but he did not attempt to engage her in conversation. Sir Neville beckoned the party outside, where grooms had brought the horses around. Althea and Jane, who had not brought any of their own horses other than the rather slow creatures that had pulled their carriage from Dettamoor Park, waited until the others had accommodated themselves and then allowed Sir Neville to lead them to the mounting block. A groom had reined in two horses, a black mare with white patches and a chestnut pony. Althea selected the pony, a pony being more appropriate for her stature.

"And what is his name?" she said to the groom, after he helped her up and she had settled her skirts over her ankles.

"Andalusia, madam."

"A very elegant name for a simple pony."

"He came with that name. Was a Spanish gentleman what owned him before."

"Oh, how very interesting. I shall have to ask Sir Neville about his history."

The group set off at an easy canter. Althea noted with some surprise that Mr. Smithson had brought with him a coal black thoroughbred that could have easily thrown a much larger man. Smithson, however, seemed perfectly at home on the animal's back and galloped ahead of the others, handling the high-strung animal with an ease that seemed alien to his normally timid demeanor.

Norwich managed to hold his large chestnut in check enough to fall in with Mrs. Gregson and Althea at the rear of the pack.

Mrs. Gregson's red hair was set off admirably by a dark green riding habit with a trim cap adorned with egret feathers. She addressed Norwich. " I wonder that Your Grace does not wish to gallop ahead with Mr. Gregson and Lord and Lady Pickney. Your horse was not made to plod along."

"I sincerely hope that that is not a hint for me to leave your charming company. My horse will do as I tell him, and I find a gentle trot is all I desire this morning."

"Of course we do not wish to chase you away. I have just been saying to Lady Trent that Ranleigh is rightly famous for its gardens and walks."

"You have been to Ranleigh before?" Norwich said.

"Sir Neville has been kind enough to invite us for several summers. He always has such charming guests. I see that Lord and Lady Batterslea have declined to join us this morning. They joined us last summer, soon after their marriage."

"I heard Batterslea say that his lady was indisposed with a headache, and he thought it better not to leave her in that state," Norwich said.

"Ah, they are still young in their marriage and cannot bear to be apart, I'm sure. They will think differently when they have been married for several years, will they not, Lady Trent?" Mrs. Gregson replied.

"Perhaps. I nursed Lord Trent through several illnesses, and so I am not a fair judge."

"Oh, illnesses yes, I understand. One does not desert a spouse in illness, but trifling headaches are not the same thing," Mrs. Gregson said.

"For some persons headaches are the very definition of illness and they suffer dreadfully," Althea replied, and then, to smooth over any awkwardness, "But I do agree that the longer one is married, the more one changes."

"In what way did you change?" Norwich said.

Althea and Mrs. Gregson looked at him, but he seemed impervious to the suggestion that his question was impertinent. Althea thought it better to answer than to challenge him, so she said, "I was married very young, so I suppose you could say that I grew into womanhood. Fortunately, Sir Arthur was a very indulgent husband who managed my girlish whims with finesse."

Mrs. Gregson smiled. "He sounds like the perfect husband! I have often observed that a kind, steady husband is worth ten handsome rakes. Young girls would do well to follow your example, Lady Trent. No end of trouble can occur when a girl marries late."

"Our marriage was a happy one," Althea agreed.

They cantered on some distance and met up with Lord and Lady Pickney. After some desultory conversation about the weather and the countryside, Norwich managed to separate Althea enough from the group for private conversation.

"I doubt very much that you had any girlish whims in need of management," he said.

"I'm not sure that I should dignify that remark with a response, as the question that proceeded it was most improper."

"I have a reputation for bluntness. Mrs. Gregson will not think the worse of me for it."

"And what if I think the worse of you?"

"Then I will beg of your forgiveness rather than stifle my own curiosity. How is it that a man like Sir Arthur was able to prevail upon a clever girl of eighteen to marry him?"

Althea colored up at the compliment. "Sir Arthur was very persuasive, in his way."

"Tell me how he went about it."

"But, dear sir, I am not the same green girl I was then. The promise of a comfortable life as a gentlewoman and the lure of science are not what they were to me when I had no idea of my future."

"But surely it cannot have been merely the offer of a comfortable life – you speak of him with such affection."

"Are you asking me if I loved my husband?"

"If I were, would you answer the question?"

Althea thought about it a moment and then said, "Yes, I will answer, and yes, I did come to love my husband. And, having had the experience of marital felicity, I will add that I cannot now contemplate a marriage without love."

"And yet you will not name the date with me. You know that I love you."

"I honor that sentiment more than I am able to express, but do not know if what I feel for you can reciprocate it."

He gave her a warm look. "Come Althea, I am too old to gammon."

"I'm sure a man of your experience knows that attraction is not the same as love."

"Aha, now we come to the point. So I have not won your heart yet?"

"I suppose not."

Althea noticed that Sir Neville had reined in his horse up ahead. The other members of the party had reined in beside him, awaiting instructions. "We shall discuss the matter further at another moment?" she said.

"Most definitely," Norwich replied.

Sir Neville soon explained the reason for the stop. He had arranged for a light picnic to be served in a glen some distance up the path and was providing his guests with instructions. The party moved on, rearranging itself so that Althea now rode beside Lady Pickney and Jane.

"I was just saying to Miss Trent how very fetching I think Mrs. Gregson's riding habit. Women with red hair can carry off positively any shade of green. One has to admire how Mrs. Gregson manages to keep it quite that shade of red – nothing faded about her – despite the fact that she came out with me in my season," Lady Pickney said.

"The women with red hair that I have known seem to have the happy knack of avoiding gray hair altogether and simply fading into blonde," Althea said.

"I think hair dye may come into play in this case," Jane said.

"My thought as well," Lady Pickney replied. "Not that I begrudge her her looks. Being married to a stiff bore like Gregson, she must have some occupation. Although I'm sure she has led her husband to believe the color is real. He is such a severe moralist that hair dye might just send him over the edge."

"I understand entirely. He was not in charity with my more flippant comments," said Althea.

Lady Pickney nodded. "His opinions are quite strict on the subject of female frailty. Mrs. Gregson didn't have much choice, I'm afraid. She was taken abroad after that first season but returned unmarried still, and so I suppose her parents despaired. Mr. Gregson must have seemed a good choice."

"Poor Mrs. Gregson." Althea said. "It must be a relief for her to get away from him now and then."

"I suppose she does what she can. In her case, I should have taken a lover long ago and been done with it," said Lady Pickney.

Jane looked a little shocked, but Althea laughed. "Perhaps that is the reason for her visit to Ranleigh."

Lady Pickney smiled. "Perhaps it is. Ah, up ahead must be the picnic Sir Neville promised. And not a minute too soon for my taste. There is something about riding that does wake up the appetite."

As Lady Pickney was quite a round lady, Althea had no trouble believing her.

The picnic was set out in a clearing at the edge of a running stream. The trees that surrounded it were clustered in such a way as to provide picturesque shade rather than dense cover. Althea brought her pony to a stop and jumped down before a servant could assist her to dismount. She handed the reins over and then walked slowly towards the blankets and cushions set out for the guests' comfort, enjoying the feel of the sun on her shoulders, the sweet smell of the grass and the feel of the warm breeze on her face. She could happily live outside during the summer. There was so much beauty in the natural world.

"A penny for your thoughts," Mrs. Gregson said, startling Althea out of her reverie.

"I was just thinking how lovely the countryside is during the summer months."

"So true. The thought of being cooped up in London at this time of year fairly makes me shudder."

"I'm sorry not to have asked before, but where do you make your home when not in London?"

"We have an estate in the north. There is also a small property in Scotland, which has been in my family for several generations. I inherited it when my father died three years ago."

"You were an only child, then?"

"Yes. All my other siblings died in childhood."

"How distressing."

"Not to me, I assure you! They were all infants and I frankly don't have much recollection of any of them. Besides, I had several cousins close to me in age and near enough to supply me with playmates."

"That is a consolation." Althea was about to inquire further when she heard a commotion from the direction they had come. It sounded like the beat of hooves on the ground. She and Mrs. Gregson both turned.

A man on horseback approached and as he got closer, Althea was able to perceive the form of Lord George Verlyn. Verlyn and Norwich shared certain features and both had an air of authority, but even those whose partiality was decided in favor of the duke had to admit that his brother was more classically handsome. He also demonstrated a more open and engaging manner, which had caused more than one lady's heart to flutter. Amongst the society gossips, it was an enduring mystery as to why Verlyn remained as yet unattached. Of course, Althea, privy to his real work on behalf of the government, could understand why Verlyn chose to steer clear of romantic entanglements. Still, it was a pity that no lady had yet stolen his heart. Althea wondered if this visit would prove definitively whether or not he had stolen hers.

Verlyn dismounted and bowed with a flourish of his hat to Althea and Mrs. Gregson. "Ladies, you have no idea what a lovely picture you make under the sylvan canopy."

Althea and Mrs. Gregson curtseyed, and Althea said, "Very pretty, my lord. How delightful that you were able to join us today. Sir Neville informed us this morning that you were coming, but I don't think we expected you quite so soon."

"The delight is all mine, I assure you."

Norwich came forward and clapped Verlyn on the back. "You made good time, brother. Come have something to eat and drink. You know most of the party, I believe."

Sir Neville approached, wreathed in smiles. "Lord George, welcome, welcome. It is an honor to have you come to Ranleigh. Please, let me offer you some refreshment."

The next half an hour was spent arranging the guests and the food to everyone's satisfaction, and when the groups were finally organized, Althea found herself sitting next to Jane and Sir Neville. As they were more attentive to each other than Althea, she was left to watch the other members of the party and to catch snippets of conversation.

Lady Pickney monopolized Verlyn with several town anecdotes, while Mrs. Gregson fought for her share of the conversation. Mr. Gregson and Lord Pickney engaged

Norwich in an apparently tedious debate about current politics. Althea could read Norwich's boredom from where she sat. Mr. Smithson sat beside Sir Neville, but because of Sir Neville's attentions to Jane, was left to look around in search of some occupation to pass the time.

He picked several blades of grass and began to braid them together. He was remarkably dexterous, Althea noted. Soon, he had a long chain of grasses that he wound around his finger and then his wrist. When he tired of this, he pulled his watch out of his pocket and began to toy with the fobs. Several of them had parts that opened or moved. Finally, he stuffed the watch back into his waistcoat. It was a fine silk waistcoat, embroidered all over with a design made up of classical columns and reclining lions. Certainly, a fanciful garment for a picnic. The design recalled a mythological story, but she couldn't put her finger on which at the moment. Her father would be so disheartened to see how her Greek had fallen off of late.

"What do you think?" Jane said to Althea.

Althea realized that she had missed some piece of conversation. "I'm sorry dear, but I've been wool gathering. Of what are we speaking?"

"Sir Neville has proposed the week after this for a visit to the seaside. How do you like the plan?"

"It is delightful. You know that I have only ever once been to the ocean, when my father made a brief visit to Burnham-on-Sea to attend a very old lady stricken with pleurisy. And even then, most of our time and efforts were spent in the sickroom. It smelled strongly of vinegar, I remember."

Jane shook her head. "My poor brother should have made more of an effort to take you about."

"No matter," Althea replied. "For I have you to drag me along on your adventures. How far is the ocean from Ranleigh?"

"Not two hours with a swift team of horses. I propose to set out early for Torquay so that we may dine at the midday and then stroll along the harbor for several hours before returning to Ranleigh for a late evening meal. How does that suit you, Lady Trent?"

"It sounds like a wonderful plan. I am all anticipation."

Sir Neville then proceeded to announce the plan to the assembled group. It was met with general approval, except for Lady Pickney, who railed against Sir Neville for wishing to encourage healthful exercise when he knew that she was not a great walker. "You shall reduce me to skin and bones with so much perambulation!" she said with a smile.

After lunch, they took advantage of the fine weather to walk along the stream. Althea stopped to admire the small quick fish darting in and out of the rocks of the bank, and Verlyn took the opportunity to approach her. He waited until the others were some distance on, and then he said, "I hear from my brother that congratulations are in order."

Althea looked up from her study and smiled at him. "Thank you. Has your brother also communicated the quiet nature of our engagement?"

Verlyn smiled in return. "He has. It seems fitting to me that he should have found the one woman in England who would hold him off. Everything comes so easily to him, you see."

Althea noticed that, despite its charm, Verlyn's smile had not accelerated her pulse perceptively and she felt a certain relief. Perhaps that flutter of excitement she had felt upon making his acquaintance originally was merely a fancy of the moment and did not portend greater attachment. "I can well perceive it. But you may be of some assistance in this matter, if you desire, for there are so many things I should like to know."

"Such as?"

"Any number of silly questions that I have not had the temerity to ask him directly. For example, what was he like as a child? Was he a kind brother?"

"Most of the time. We fought, like all brothers do, particularly when he sought to assert his authority over me. I remember that, on one occasion, I shoved him into the lake in a fit of pique. Fortunately, he could swim, unlike the late baron."

"You are very close, I perceive."

"As close as we can be given my travels. But, may I usurp this conversation to ask for a description of how you found Lord Tunwell? I fear I may not have many opportunities for private conversation with you."

"Of course." Althea relayed the story, and when she was done, she added, "Your brother has the paper with him. We think it may be a map."

"You may be right. Is there any place we could meet to discuss the matter with my brother when we return to the house?"

"There are some secluded walks in the rose garden. If one were to meet at an appointed time, a private meeting might be arranged."

"Then I shall make arrangements. Now that that is settled, what other deep dark secrets do you desire to know about your betrothed?"

"Only the deepest and darkest, I assure you," Althea replied archly.

CHAPTER ELEVEN

Later that afternoon, Norwich, Verlyn and Althea all found excuses to tour the roses. They met up at the end of a path, surrounded on three sides by large fragrant bushes.

"And how did you know about this secluded location?" Norwich asked Althea. His tone implied a certain level of suspicion.

"My knowledge is innocently acquired, I assure you. I find I cannot sleep past a certain hour of the morning and have taken to walking the grounds of Ranleigh. Besides, Jane and Sir Neville are often to be found here."

Verlyn laughed. "Sir Neville was right to bring her to Ranleigh. Few women could resist such beauty and fragrance. It is most romantic."

"I know of at least one," remarked Norwich. "But let us get down to business. Althea, I assume you have given George the particulars of your discovery of the paper?"

Althea nodded.

Norwich pulled out his watch and flipped open the back. He handed the paper to Verlyn. "What do you make of that?"

Verlyn examined the paper carefully. "It looks like it might be a map." He stared at the lines again. "Or perhaps a code of some sort."

"If I may be permitted to ask, how long had the baron been under suspicion?" Althea said.

"Some months. He had friends in high places, and when we discovered that certain information had been leaked, Lord Tunwell was the logical candidate to have received it and passed it on," Verlyn said.

"So you think his death was not an accident?" Althea said.

"It may have been or it may not. I cannot tell at this point," Verlyn replied.

"One wonders, *cui bono?*"

Verlyn nodded thoughtfully.

"What would you have us do?" Norwich said.

"Nothing for now, except to observe our fellow guests."

"Is there something in particular we should be on the lookout for?" Althea said.

"No, but I would be interested to know of any behavior that is out of the ordinary. Sir Neville plans a day expedition to Torquay, I gather. Ranleigh's proximity to the harbor may hold some importance. Some portion of the fleet has been in port there since the war began," Verlyn said.

Althea nodded. "If Tunwell's death was not an accident, then the murderer must be one of the party or someone familiar with the estate. Likely someone the baron knew, because there would be no way to approach that section of the pond without being detected. The harbor at Torquay merely provides yet another mechanism of approach, assuming the assassin was not of the Ranleigh party. He could have escaped by boat, if he desired."

"I admit that I find it hard to imagine anyone of our party a murderer," Norwich said. "Anyone except Cruikshank, of course."

"Cruikshank was here?" Verlyn said.

Norwich nodded. "He came to claim the body."

"Nasty fellow. He might be capable of anything," Verlyn said.

"Would someone please enlighten me as to why Mr. Cruikshank is held in such abhorrence? Other than scandalous behavior with women and propensity to spend money he doesn't have, which my brief time in London would indicate is not that unusual, I have a hard time seeing him as a murderer," Althea said.

"Don't let that pretty face fool you," Verlyn replied. "Apart from those vices you have named, you can add cheating at cards, dealing in contraband, and swindling green young men to your list."

"Those are certainly heavy charges," Althea said, "but what would make a man like that stoop to murder? And why now, when his uncle is staying at another man's house?

Surely, a murder in London would be much more convenient for Cruikshank?"

"But a murder in London has two disadvantages. The first is that Cruikshank would be easily suspected. He has lived on the expectations of his inheritance for years. The second is that Bow Street might have been called in to investigate," Norwich said.

"Those are indeed disadvantages," Althea admitted. Both she and Norwich had been privileged to work for Bow Street and so knew of the very extensive surveillance networks established by Mr. Read, the magistrate. "But if Cruikshank traveled to Ranleigh for the purpose of murdering his uncle, then we should be able to trace his movements. He would have stopped somewhere to rest his horses when going both to and from the country. Would he have had time to kill his uncle and then be back in London when the courier reached him with the news? For he couldn't be sure of when the body would be found."

"From your examination, when do you think the baron was killed?" Norwich said to Althea.

"Did you examine the body?" Verlyn said with surprise.

Althea looked at Norwich, but he refrained from comment. "Yes, I was able to do a cursory examination. Given the state of rigidity of the body, I would say he died that morning. Was Lord Tunwell usually an early riser?"

"I'm sure I don't know. Why?" Norwich asked.

"If he was, his murderer might have followed him to the pond. If he wasn't, then it is more likely to have been a prearranged assignation. Also, Sir Neville mentioned that he had seen the baron at breakfast, and Sir Neville is not particularly early to the breakfast table. Lord George, are you aware if any of the other guests are in a position to help his majesty's government, like you are?"

"You think he was killed by one of us?" Verlyn said.

"Only a thought."

Verlyn smiled ruefully. "I wish I was in full possession of that knowledge. However, the powers that be feel that it is dangerous for one man to know too much about other operations. I know enough to manage my own affairs, no more."

"But you wouldn't have been allowed to join us here if the government thought there was any conflict with your investigation of Tunwell's death, correct?" Norwich said.

"They raised no objection to me coming here. In fact, they welcomed the idea."

"Do they know about the paper in the watch fob?" Althea said.

"No. I wasn't sure what to tell them until I had seen it myself. And given the vague nature of the communication, I'm not sure what to say to the Home Office."

"Far be it from me to tell you your business, brother, but I might wait to make that communication until we have a better idea of what we are dealing with. The paper may be important, or it may not."

"That was my thought," Verlyn replied. He pulled out his watch. "I suggest that we make our way back to the house before our collective absence is remarked upon. I shall ride out tomorrow on some pretext and make inquiries related to Cruikshank's movements. Let me leave now, for the rumors are already rampant about you and Lady Trent. I would hate to add to them the idea that she has ensnared the hearts of us both." He turned, gave a jaunty wave, and walked back in the direction of the house.

When he was out of earshot, Norwich said, "I'm glad we have a moment alone. I have been desiring speech with you."

"To what end?" Althea said.

"I'm sure I don't need to reiterate my position, but this is another matter. I had a message from my sister when we returned to the house that mother is suffering a new illness, congestion of the lungs."

"Oh dear, I hope that she is not seriously ill? My father always recommended a steam bath in such cases."

"Reading between the lines, I think she is likely to have exaggerated its severity. However, I have instructed Minerva to write me immediately should she worsen. I didn't want to mention it in front of George because heaven knows he would be likely to dash off to Bath, filled with regret, and that might not be at all in the nation's best interest. My mother can be very persuasive and thinks quite highly of her own complaints. She has George convinced that it was his absence that gave our father an apoplexy, which is quite ridiculous, but very much her style. So, my poor brother lives wracked with guilt every time he has to leave the country."

"How very unfortunate. In my experience, apoplexy may occur at any time and has more to do with a heavy diet and a lack of exercise than apprehension at a son's travel abroad. But I take from this that you and your sister try to manage your mother's health without unduly alarming your brother?"

"Yes, so I would appreciate your discretion. I merely wanted to mention it to you because I may be forced to leave suddenly if her illness turns out to be more than a trifling thing."

"I appreciate the warning, but surely you know that I would not take any attentions to your mother amiss?"

"No, of course not. Anyone who loved her father as you loved yours would understand. It is merely that I had hoped to tell her about our engagement. She despairs of me ever marrying, and this news would certainly bring her back from the portals of death, if she heard it."

Althea looked at him with an air of innocence. "By all means, tell her what you would like. I think we agreed to tell our close family, did we not?"

Norwich's eyes flashed. "I would not seek to put my future wife at such a disadvantage. My mother is very strict in her notions of propriety and an engagement on trial will not be at all acceptable. She will think I have gone mad to agree to such a thing."

"I see. And what will you think?"

"I am beginning to think that you deliberately put me off. Please, for the love of God, tell me that you will give me a straight answer if I have to ask you for it."

"I suppose I shall, although I never thought my hand would be forced in such a manner. It does take all of the romance out of the thing."

"Is that why you torment me? For the romance of it?" he said angrily.

Now it was Althea's turn for a sharp look. "I loathe to give anyone pain, but I think you fail to understand just what it means to me to have finally achieved a position where I may do as I like and go where I please, and where I am free to pursue my own interests without interference. I have lived all my life under the watchful eyes of my father and then my husband. And, although I loved them both, I find my new-found independence quite invigorating. I'm sure that such hesitation seems ridiculous to a man who has always lived as he chooses, but please grant me the luxury of time enough to make a decision that I shall not soon regret. Do not push me too hard. *Hic manebimus optime!*"

"While your Latin is impeccable, I promise you'll have no regrets." Norwich replied, pulling her to him so quickly that she had no time to object. His lips found hers in a ruth-less kiss.

I shall lose all my power to resist, Althea thought, as she fell deeper under the spell of his intoxicating persuasion. Her arms found their way around his neck, and she burrowed into his embrace, unable to restrain the flame of desire that sprang up within her. It was dangerous, but so wickedly compelling.

Finally, Althea gathered her wits and tried to pull away. "Sir, I beg of you," she said. "Release me and I shall give you my answer if you have need of it. I promise."

His eyes remained unfocused as he studied her, seeming not to hear her words. Then he let go of her and stepped back. "Good," he said gruffly. "I must return to the house." And with that, he turned on his heel and left her standing bewildered amongst the rose bushes.

CHAPTER TWELVE

When Althea returned, she met a flustered Miss Dorkins, who told her quite plainly what she thought of mistresses arriving too late to be properly dressed for dinner.

"I have been walking amongst the rose bushes," Althea replied, with some asperity. "They are the crown jewel of the gardens of Ranleigh."

"I'm sure that there was very little walking and much more digging around in the bushes looking for insects. You cannot hide your rumpled appearance from me, Lady Trent. I don't know how I will get those creases out of your dress. It will simply take ages!"

Althea decided that insect investigations were certainly preferable to the real cause of her wrinkles and so closed her mouth diplomatically. Miss Dorkins continued to mutter on about this and that until Althea sat down in her petticoats so that Dorkins could assist her to remove her boots.

"Oh my, look at how they are caked with mud. I shall have to send them down to be cleaned and heaven knows when we shall get them back again. They have no notion of how to manage things in this household. Why, they sent up a pair of boots that weren't even yours this afternoon, and I have yet to discover who they might belong to because the under housemaid would insist that they belonged to you, although it was clear as a pikestaff that they didn't – your boots being ever so much smaller."

"Really?" Althea replied as a curtesy. Many years of experience had given her practice in appearing to follow Miss Dorkins' conversation without paying her the least mind.

"Look at these." Dorkins handed her a boot. "I cannot imagine what she was thinking, for they are not in the least like yours."

Althea dutifully examined the boot thrust at her. It was made of a dark brown leather, with a hard leather sole and a small stacked heel. She turned it over, noticing that the under housemaid had not cleaned it thoroughly because a piece of plant matter stuck out from underneath the layers of the heel. A banded horsetail, by the look of it. She handed the boot back to Miss Dorkins. "I hope they find their owner, for they seem a good sturdy pair of boots. Just the thing to walk all over Ranleigh."

"It is a good thing that I packed several pairs of boots for you, Lady Trent, or else you would be left with your satin slippers."

"Which I would be sure to ruin with my explorations. Yes, I understand what a trial I must be to you, dear Miss Dorkins."

"Who is a trial?" Jane entered the room without ceremony.

"Me, of course. Jane, how lovely you look with that cream satin gown. A rose from the gardens as a posy is all that you need to make you look like a blushing school girl."

Jane laughed. "You know I pay you no mind, Althea, so you can leave off with your mendacious comments."

"See how I am insulted and abused, Miss Dorkins? But seriously, Jane, I think Ranleigh agrees with you, for you have a glow now that I haven't seen in many years."

"I think it must be all the fresh air and exercise," Jane said dismissively. "Now please hurry up or we will be late to dinner."

"We wouldn't want that, although I must say that since Cruikshank left us, we have not had quite the same thrill of dangerous conversation at our end of the table."

"You don't find Mr. Gregson dangerous?" Jane said with a smile.

"No, although I will admit that Mrs. Gregson puzzles me."

Miss Dorkins handed Althea into a pale-yellow gown with green embroidery.

Jane shrugged. "She seems common enough to me."

"She told me that she had no sadness for all of her siblings who died as children. That seems to me an odd sort of statement to make. It paints her as rather cold and not a little ruthless."

"I suppose so, but the death of children is not so very uncommon. You are blessed that young Arthur is such a fine strong young man."

"I have seen many dead children and wept for them even as they were my father's patients and strangers to me. But I suppose others may not take death as I do."

"You seem far more comfortable than most, Althea. I saw no tears for Lord Tunwell."

"Adults yes, for I am not at all squeamish. But there is something about persons who have had no chance to experience life that I find terribly affecting. In any case, it was merely an observation and may not indicate anything in particular."

Mercifully for Miss Dorkin's peace of mind, the ladies were not the last to arrive and Althea was spared a sharp scold. Althea was escorted in to dinner by Mr. Gregson and followed his inconsequential chatter for the course of the meal. Althea had to admit that his superior manner rankled just a little bit. He was just like every other man of his ilk, satisfied in his own opinions. She caught Verlyn's eye at one point by the merest chance, but his quick understanding of her boredom brought a smile to her lips that was answered by one of his own.

Lord George Verlyn had a delightful smile, Althea decided, and she tested its effect on her. There had been a point where such a smile would have stirred a fluttering of her heart, but she noticed that it produced a feeling of warmth and silent camaraderie now, not the stirrings of a more carnal nature. Those desires seemed to have been entirely reserved for his brother, who sat in brooding silence at the end of the table. Althea supposed that silence was preferable to flirtatious conversation with Lady Batterslea, but it was obvious that he was still in an unsettled mood.

After dinner, Jane offered to play some music for dancing and Althea readily agreed to Lord George's invitation to take a turn. Norwich declined to participate, but instead took up a position by the piano, where he watched the proceedings and maintained desultory conversation with Jane.

"I fear your brother is not in charity with me at the moment," Althea said.

"I'm sure it cannot be of long duration. My brother's temper is quick but not resentful."

"No indeed, but I fear he must often have his way for true happiness." And then because Norwich's sulking was such a lowering thought, she said, "Tell me another story. What was his favorite pastime as a child?"

"He was forever wandering about the house with his nose in a book. It put me all out of patience with him whenever I needed him to build a kite or some other much more exciting activity."

"So he was not fond of athletic pursuits?"

"He was fond of them, particularly riding, but ideas were his real passion. Still are. I don't know that I have ever met with someone as well read."

"Indeed. I remarked upon it when we first met."

Lord George smiled. "He mentioned that you had wide literary tastes."

"We are certainly well matched in that regard."

Later that evening, after Miss Dorkins had prepared Althea for bed, Althea sat by the dying embers of the small fire so thoughtfully lit in the guests' bedrooms. She'd been mulling over her potential frog study, the baron, and her troubles with Norwich when Jane entered from the antechamber.

"A penny for your thoughts?" Jane said.

"Just thinking of the pond frogs. And you?"

"I suppose the same thing," Jane said.

"I never pictured you a naturalist."

"Your father did not have the time or inclination to tell you stories, did he?"

"What do you mean?"

"Magical stories about princesses and far off lands. Specifically, a certain story about a prince turned into a frog," Jane said.

"And how does one make him a prince?" Althea asked.

"By kissing him, of course."

"Ah, but can the heroine be sure he will become a prince? Perhaps he is just a frog."

"That is the rub," Jane replied. "And what about your frog? Is he a prince?"

"According to his brother, he is the best of men. No webbed feet."

"It sounds as if you do not quite believe the reports." Jane sank into the chair opposite Althea.

"I suppose I have had it too much to my liking since Arthur's death. Do you not fear the loss of your independence, Jane?"

"An unmarried woman, even one of my age, can never be really considered independent. Our status in society is too low for that. Still, I do fear leaving Dettamoor Park and all that is dear to me."

"Perhaps that is the cause of my hesitation as well." Althea sighed. "Let us talk of pleasanter things."

"Such as?"

"Light gossip, perhaps. I noticed that Mr. Gregson, despite his strictures on female morality, was most attentive to Lady Batterslea. He danced with her twice, I believe."

"Three times, but we are a small party, so that accounts for it. Mr. Smithson is quite an elegant dancer. So light upon his feet."

"Yes. He is quite surprising. Do you know anything about him? I fear I know nothing more than what he told me himself."

"He is from Yorkshire and has been upon the town these last ten years or more."

Althea nodded. "Sir Neville must have a penchant for persons of a northern orientation. Counting the late baron, there are three of our party that hail from the North."

Jane nodded. "That is an odd coincidence. Although you would never know it by the polish of their speech."

"No indeed. Especially Mr. Smithson. From what I can gather, he is the sort of man to be invited everywhere and by everyone. But single men usually are. Is there no gossip about potential marriage partners? A single man with an independence must have had many young women thrust in his way."

"No one ever mentioned anything along those lines. Perhaps his fortune is more modest than he advertises. He could be nothing but debt, for all we know."

"He certainly spends a sum on dress. His waistcoats are beyond anything. Particularly that one with the lions and the pillars. What is the mythological reference, do you know? I swear I should know it but cannot pull it out of my muddled brain."

Jane laughed. "If you cannot make it out, I am certain I cannot. You are the scholar in the family."

Althea chuckled. "A poor one if I have forgotten all my Greek mythology. So it is set we are to make a grand expedition to Torquay?"

"Yes. I think it shall be just the thing to alleviate the pall that has settled since Lord Tunwell's accidental death."

"If indeed it was an accident."

"Don't tell me that you have taken it into your head to investigate? Please Althea, Sir Neville is justly concerned enough as it is without causing more of a scene."

"I promise I won't cause any unpleasantness."

CHAPTER THIRTEEN

And indeed Althea was true to her word for the next several days, managing to while the time away in long walks and pond studies. These were frequently interrupted by a most unlikely cause. Lord George Verlyn was also apparently a great enthusiast for the natural splendors of Ranleigh, and he and Althea often crossed paths. He seemed to take a keen interest in her pond frog observations, even going so far as to help her by holding some of the reeds apart so that she could peer into their watery habitat.

Their conversations were not all about science, however. On one of these occasions, Althea took the opportunity to quiz him on his inquiries related to Cruikshank.

"I can find no evidence that he was anywhere in the vicinity prior to his uncle's death," Verlyn said.

"Well, that is disappointing, I'm sure. Although he may have been a master of stealth, and able to avoid the village gossips."

"He would have to have been with that handsome face he has. My experience with the fairer sex would lead me to believe that his appearance in a small village would be memorable."

Althea looked up from her scribbled notes. "Do I detect a note of jealousy in your voice, Lord George?"

"No, I do not have a jealous nature. I have seen too much misery at his hands, however, to like the man."

"Misery of the kind you mentioned before – gaming and debauchery?"

"And something of a more personal nature. My cousin, now Lady Graves, was entranced by him and then cruelly and publicly repelled. A woman with less sense would have gone into a decline after such treatment."

"I am so very sorry to hear that. But as he had dubious prospects, her parents must have been somewhat relieved that the match did not move forward."

"My parents certainly were. Isabel was in their keeping since her parents died some years ago of the influenza."

"So she has grown up with her cousins?"

"Yes, you might say that. She is two years younger than my sister."

"Then all's well that ends well, I suppose, if she is now Lady Graves."

"Graves is a decent enough young man. Perhaps a little too young to be a proper husband, but after all that passed with Cruikshank, we could not deny her."

"And what is the suitable age for a husband?" Althea asked, smiling.

"Exactly my brother's age, I think." He smiled in return.

Althea looked down and then, because her curiosity got the better of her, casually said, "What of yourself, my lord? Has no lady tempted you to resign your bachelor state?"

Verlyn paused before speaking, and Althea looked up, regarding him carefully.

"I don't know that I am a fit person for marriage," he said with a certain melancholy, "at least, I don't think I'd be a very good husband in my present position. There have been several ladies I regarded with admiration, but no eligible lady who could tempt me to give up my occupation, which I would be obliged to do."

"Yes, I can well understand," Althea said, catching his emphasis on the word *eligible*, and understanding that a lost love was at the root of his present solitude. "And one should hold out for love, if one has the choice to do so."

"Exactly my thought. Have you taken the notes you need?"

"One moment more, if you would be so kind." Althea stepped forward and felt her boot squish into the mud. She disregarded it, and peered deeper into the marsh grass. A small speckled frog stared back at her and then hopped blithely away. When she finally extricated herself, she found her petticoats had a nice ring of filth. "Oh dear," she said, as she stared at her mud-caked shoes. "Miss Dorkins will have my head!"

Verlyn laughed. "You must tell her it was all in the name of science. I'm sure she will understand."

Althea shook her head. "That excuse is threadbare. But there is no helping it. I will just have to take my lumps."

Verlyn offered her his arm and they set off back towards the house. They were just coming up the drive, and Althea was just deciding on the best mechanism to placate Miss Dorkins, when a thought occurred to her. She quickly thanked Verlyn for his good offices and headed to her room.

"Miss Dorkin's?" she said, as she opened the door.

"Yes, Lady Trent?" Dorkins emerged from her lair between the rooms.

"What happened to those boots you showed me before?"

"I still have them because none of the other servants would claim them. Likely no one wishes to take the blame for misplacing them."

"May I see the boots? And before you say anything else, I know that my dress and petticoat are a horror of tremendous proportions."

"To say nothing of your own boots, my lady. Caked in mud they are! Do please sit so that I may help you to remove them."

"Yes." Althea sat down. "But do not take them away just yet. I want to do a comparison."

When she was in her stocking feet, she took the stranger's boot that had the pieces of banded horsetail and one of her own over to the window. "Bring me my portable writing desk, if you will."

She set the desk and the boots on the floor and then extracted a piece of paper and the knife used to trim her quill pens. She bent down and ran the blade of the knife between the heel and the sole of the stranger's boot, dislodging the reed and bits of dark gray soil. She did the same with her own boots on a second piece of paper and then handed her boots to Dorkins. "They are all yours, my dear Miss Dorkins."

"And what do you mean to do with those dirty pieces of paper?"

"I shall let the dirt from my boots dry out and then I will fold the paper thus," she folded the other paper over the dirt until it made a little envelope, "and I will mark it so that when I examine the other envelopes, I shall know which is which."

Dorkins shook her head. "I will never understand your experiments, Lady Trent, but then again I have long resigned myself to your strange ways. Just please have pity on the poor laundress, I beg of you."

Althea smiled. "I promise, dear Miss Dorkins. I shall have a care to the best of my ability. Here, please help me to remove the dress and these petticoats."

Later that afternoon, Althea joined Jane, Lady Batterslea and Mrs. Gregson on a sojourn to Berryfield, the small village a mile or two beyond the gates of Ranleigh. Althea would have preferred to walk, but Jane, seconded by Mrs. Gregson, asked for the carriage. The village was typical of many country villages in that it consisted of a large, rather muddy road running through the middle of it, lined with small shops and traversed by carriages and carts of every description. The Ranleigh carriage was certainly one of the more elegant ones, and Lady Batterslea made a face as the coachman pulled the equipage in beside a farmer's wagon in front of a shop that seemed to be a purveyor of marzipan and other sweet things. The sign over the door read *Manton's Confectioners.*

"I feel like we are at the ends of the earth here in Berryfield. It is so rustic!" Lady Batterslea said, with an affected lilt to her voice.

Althea met Jane's gaze, but refrained from comment.

"I think country villages are delightful," said Mrs. Gregson. "There is such a purity of spirit to be found, nothing of affectation or dissimulation. And you must admit that we had many a fine afternoon eating marzipan at Mrs. Manton's here when we all visited Ranleigh last summer."

"Yes, Manton's is delightful, but you must admit that country shops are nothing to what can be found almost anywhere else. I was saying as much to the duke last evening, and he quite agreed with me. When one has access to London, one cannot stoop to accept what the provincials deem is fine."

The coachman opened the carriage door and the ladies stepped onto the packed earth of the street, augmented here and there with planks of wood. Lady Batterslea and Mrs. Gregson declared a desire to taste the marzipan directly, but Althea, spying both a book seller and an apothecary shop across the way said to Jane, "Won't you come with me to explore a bit? The walk would do us both good."

Jane agreed, and it was decided that the ladies would meet back at the confectioner's shop in an hour in order to return to Ranleigh.

Once they were out of earshot, Althea said, "I'm afraid I find Lady Batterslea's discourse a bit tiresome." She took Jane's arm and crossed over to the book seller.

"There is certainly plenty of it. For such a young lady, she has an extensive number of opinions."

"Please tell me that I was not like her when I married your brother."

Jane chuckled. "No, my dear. You had many opinions, but they were the product of a sound education. Poor Lady Batterslea is destined to become another one of London's flighty and ill-informed matrons. Proof yet again that a little beauty thrown in the right direction is all a lady needs for success."

"A certain kind of success." Althea continued on lightly as if she had no concerns. "Poor Norwich. How he must suffer her company."

Jane frowned and opened the door to the shop. Upon closer examination, it was less a purveyor of books than a shop dedicated to any number of useful items, from writing paper to weights for commercial scales. The books on offer consisted of various copies of the Bible and assorted sermons. There were also several popular novels of dubious value, most concerned with stories of the dark and mysterious type or overwrought heroines such as Richardson's *Pamela*.

Althea greeted the young man behind the counter and asked if he had any books of a scientific nature. When he could produce nothing but a popular almanac, Althea gave up thoughts of a book and turned instead to a small display of seals and sealing wax. She held up a red wax bar. "What do you think of this, Jane? I have run through my widow's black wax. Do you think red suits me?"

Jane came over to her. "I think so. Not that red sealing wax marks you as particularly daring."

"Am I thought daring?"

"Unusual, certainly. Would you take it amiss if I drop a word of warning in your ear?"

"Do you mean, would I do the opposite just because I have been warned?"

Jane smiled ruefully. "Yes, I suppose I mean that."

"But you will warn me no matter what I respond, so please tell me what I should refrain from."

Jane lowered her voice so that the clerk wouldn't overhear them. "It is less to prevent you from action, than to repeat an observation. A man with the best intentions may yet be led astray by the excessive flattery of a young pretty woman. Particularly, one who seems bound and determined to make a conquest."

Althea looked down, trying valiantly to control her expression. There was no need to let Jane know that Althea shared Jane's concerns. "I am assuming you mean His Grace and Lady Batterslea?"

"Yes, Althea, I do. I may be a spinster, but credit me with some perspicacity. Although he may not mean for a romance to occur, women of Lady Batterslea's stamp will stop at nothing to achieve their end. And the conquest of a duke, however short-lived, is still a notable thing."

Althea looked at Jane defiantly. "And what if she does? It is none of my business if he engages in a dalliance. As a fiancée or even a wife, I am supposed to ignore anything he chooses to do. Isn't that what society tells us poor women?"

"You know that is not how you feel."

Althea sighed. "To be frank with you, dear sister, I am not sure how I feel at the moment."

"I have said too much already. Come, will you purchase the wax or not?"

Althea purchased the wax and then dragged Jane with her into the apothecary shop. Her temper needed the calming influence of conversation with like-minded persons. She was in luck, because the apothecary himself attended the counter. They chatted amicably for several minutes about popular remedies. Then Althea asked about a senna preparation that she had promised to secure for Miss Dorkins, who often suffered from the stomach ache. As Althea went to pull some coins from her reticule to pay for it, she noticed a selection of comfits.

"And what flavors do you have?" she said.

The apothecary was an elderly gentleman with a set of bushy white whiskers. He ran his hand down his chin in a contemplative way and replied, "My wife makes them up. Let me see." He squinted at the little round balls laid neatly in rows on a long tray. "Anise and mint and those white ones should be almond. They are my good wife's own recipe and very popular."

Althea pointed to the almond ones. They were exactly like the one she had found in the pond. "I'd like twenty of those, please. And would you happen to know if a tall gentleman bought some of the almond comfits perhaps a fortnight ago? He was a well-dressed gentleman, staying at Ranleigh."

"You mean the one that drowned in the pond?"

"Yes, the very same. Someone mentioned that you were called out when the body was discovered." Althea said.

The apothecary nodded. "I reviewed Lord Tunwell's body and recognized him immediately from the day before when he visited the shop to purchase the comfits."

"Such a sad business, him drowning that way. I assume it was accidental?"

"Yes, that was my opinion."

"You wouldn't happen to know if he purchased something other than the comfits that day?"

"Just the comfits. He said he preferred the almond ones above anything. And he mentioned that he had his medicine prepared in London, so I didn't press him, although we are known far and wide for the invigorating tonics we prepare. They will do wonders for any ailment known to God and man."

Althea smiled. "Then I shall certainly be back if I fall ill." She paid the apothecary and left the shop with Jane.

They examined some tired-looking bonnets in a storefront on the opposite side of the street. Jane seemed careful not to mention the topic of their previous conversation, but instead focused her sharp tongue on a particularly sad confection made of woven straw. When bonnet criticism began to pall, they walked slowly back to join the other ladies and inspect the marzipan. It was glossy and sweet and formed in such a way that it might almost have been real fruit, the designs were so true to life. Althea and Jane bought several for themselves and then had a package made up special for Miss Dorkins.

When they returned to Ranleigh, Miss Dorkins was in a transport of delight with both the marzipan and the senna tonic, and Althea hoped that they might be mutually beneficial. Before these transports caused Miss Dorkins to indulge in an excess of coddling, however, Althea removed her own boots, turned them over and scraped the dirt from between the sole and the heel onto a clean sheet of paper, folded it and then wrote *Streets of Berryfield* in large letters across it. She put the paper with the others in her armoire and waited for Miss Dorkins to assist her to change for the afternoon.

Things were now at a pass that Althea felt the need for advice. After Miss Dorkins was finished with her work, Althea retrieved her writing desk and composed a missive outlining all of the facts she had gathered to date related to the death of the baron. She filled fully two pages crossed once over with her neat handwriting and then addressed the whole to Mr. James Read, Magistrate of Bow Street. She sealed the missive with her new red wax and set it aside to have Sir Neville frank it for her. Apart from her beloved father, Althea had not met with another man who had so easily accepted her for her talents alone as Mr. Read. It was a comfort to know that no matter how strange Althea's letter must seem, Magistrate Read was sure to take the matter seriously. Her mind traveled to the matter of the Duke of Norwich. He had once seemed to admire her for her intellect.

CHAPTER FOURTEEN

A s if to confirm the dispiriting nature of her thoughts,
Althea and the duke saw each other frequently for
the next week, but each time they met, Althea could sense
that a cold distance had settled over the relationship. She
fought to ignore it, and sought refuge in light-hearted
conversation with Lord George, who was only too happy
to oblige her with a full measure of his attention. And although she didn't want to credit that a man of Norwich's
erudition and intelligence could be led astray by a bubble-
headed simpleton, she noticed every arch look and encouraging word Lady Batterslea threw in his direction. Lord
Batterslea noticed it as well and often sat with a glum expression as his wife prattled happily along. Lady Pickney,
that choice observer of her fellow men, summed it up best
when she said that Lady Batterslea was like a horsefly, small

but annoyingly effective. "She will sting whoever swats at her, mark my words," she added.

And so it was with some relief that Althea awoke on the morning of the visit to Torquay. At least a day at the seaside would provide some relief from the tension of the house party. Althea allowed Miss Dorkins to convince her to wear a new muslin day dress she had not had the occasion to put on before. It was block printed with a sprawling flower design in shades of indigo. Althea topped it with a green spencer, buttoned high up the throat, that she knew set off her dark hair and brown eyes. She chose a straw bonnet to accompany the outfit and one of her larger parasols to protect her complexion.

Jane, who was awake and dressed much earlier than she was accustomed, met Althea in the breakfast parlor. "You do look very smart, my dear."

"As do you, dear Jane. I must admit that I am giddy as a school girl and have every expectation of the day being very fine."

"I think Sir Neville has arranged the whole thing to perfection. He seems to have a knack for arranging social functions."

"Much to be admired in a husband."

Jane merely smiled and asked Althea to pass the butter.

They were soon joined by other guests, and the breakfast parlor became so crowded that Althea slipped away and sought refuge in the library. She had a mind to waste a half an hour in browsing the shelves by herself, but when she opened the door, she surprised Mr. Smithson. He had been standing near a window, reading what looked to be a half sheet of paper when she came in. The paper was stuffed hastily in his waistcoat pocket and he made a move to turn towards the window and then slowly turned back.

"Ah, Lady Trent, I think the day will be quite fine. There are some clouds to the east, but I do not perceive that they are at all a cause for alarm."

"No indeed. I am sorry to disturb you, Mr. Smithson. I have just come from a very noisy breakfast and thought I might catch a few moments repose with a book."

"Then do not let me detain you. I too have breakfasted. Although I will say that were it not for the sake of my dear friend, Sir Neville, I would not have bestirred myself at this ungodly hour. In any case, I thought to discern the potential weather hazards, but seeing none, suppose that I should ready myself for the rigors of the journey." He took a step towards the door. "I understand that you are to take Lord and Lady Pickney with you in your carriage. I'm sure that will be quite a lively party."

Althea wasn't sure if Smithson meant that remark seriously or not, but she let him pass by her and out of the room.

It was indeed a lively party. Traveling in their coach towards the tail of the carriage caravan, Lady Pickney did her best to entertain them all with bubbly conversation. Lord Pickney smiled at her indulgently and patted her hand every now and again. It was a picture of domestic felicity that made Althea just the least bit nostalgic for times gone by. Perhaps marriage to Norwich would result in just such a level of contentment, but given their strong temperaments, she doubted it. No, if they married, she could foresee a tempestuous union.

Torquay was a beautiful city, laid out in a half moon shape around the deep harbor. The rugged hills that surrounded the city contained a spider web of paths and small thatched cottages hanging from the hillsides. The buildings of Torquay proper were large and seemingly new, constructed of brick and stone. Althea could see several good size inns and more than half a dozen shops along the main thoroughfare. It seemed a comely place to pass a summer's day.

There was a yellow sand beach down by the water and walking paths that led down to it from the streets above. A long pier jutted out into the harbor, and various dinghies and small fishing boats were moored to it. Farther out in the harbor, two large frigates stood watchful guard.

The sun glinted off the waves. There was a breeze blowing, evidenced by the way the flags on the frigates swung to and fro. It was strong enough to whip the ladies' skirts about and ruffle their hair. Althea smiled to herself. Lady Batterslea was sure to have plenty to complain about.

The group decided to take a turn along the harbor path beside the beach before adjourning to an inn for a substantial repast. Sir Neville had promised fine food and the best ale this side of London. As the party disembarked, Althea felt a rush of excitement. She had forgotten the briny deliciousness of the smell of the ocean. It made her feel giddy and alive. She inhaled another deep breath and turned her face up to feel the sun on her skin for a brief moment. Nature was wondrous and divine.

"And what might that smile mean?" a voice close to her said.

She turned to Verlyn. "I find the sea air most agreeable, do you not?"

"Most agreeable, except when I am on a ship, and then I find myself turned into the worst sort of invalid. It is very wounding to my pride."

Althea laughed. "At least you have had the experience to know. I have never set foot on anything bigger than a row boat."

"I'm sure you would have a stronger stomach than I do. My brother tells me that nothing seems to perturb you. Even the sight of a corpse did nothing to shatter your unflappable calm."

"So he told you about that, did he? I never imagined that unflappability was such an attractive quality."

"One among many."

Althea studied him a moment. "I wonder." She looked fleetingly at Lady Batterslea, who at the moment was laughing at something Mr. Gregson had said. "Perhaps good humor and flattery might be more acceptable qualities in a woman."

Verlyn caught her look. "A man of understanding would never trade insipid laughter for a true meeting of the minds."

"Yes, of course. And your brother has a prodigious understanding."

Jane approached at that moment and took Althea's arm. "Shall we begin our stroll?"

"By all means."

The group ambled along in twos and threes until they reached the path that led to the beach. Althea and Jane were accompanied by Verlyn, who maintained an innocuous flow of conversation about the current sunshine and the prospect for fine weather.

Their progress was hampered by the breeze that required the ladies to hold on to their skirts so as not to be tripped by the fabric. At one point, Althea heard a chuckle behind her, and turning, encountered the amused gaze of Norwich. She was at a loss to understand his amusement and then it occurred to her that the wind was pressing the fabric of all of the ladies' muslin gowns very tightly to their legs. *I suppose we must all of us look quite indecent,* she thought nervously, and then, because the thought of her as a wanton *femme fatal* seemed completely absurd, she threw back her head and laughed aloud.

"A penny for your thoughts," Norwich said, suddenly close behind her.

"Stand back sir, I'm sure the view is much better at the end of the line," Althea replied, pausing so as to fall behind Verlyn and Jane.

He came up on her other side. "Indeed," he said with a wry smile, "but I find that I crave your conversation more."

"Well, I have never ceased to talk."

"No, you haven't." He was quiet then and Althea studied him, trying to discern the nature of his current mood. He had been so distant of late that she longed to say something in order to sustain the conversation, but she didn't know quite what to say.

"I gather from my brother that these ships we see are but a small portion of this ships that are sometimes moored here," he said, obviously making an effort to find a neutral topic of conversation.

"The Admiralty must be a great boon to the town," Althea replied.

"I think that the Navy is the town for most of the summer."

"We certainly have much to thank the Navy for."

"The naval men of my acquaintance are as fine a set of fellows as you will ever meet," Norwich replied.

"I'm afraid I have very limited experience with the Navy. I know that my father attended an Admiral or two, but for the most part, he was only called in when they were nothing short of death. Apparently, they did not have much interest in treatment until it couldn't be helped."

"That fits with my experience, as well. They are not the sort to fancy themselves ill."

Althea was about to reply when Jane said, "Look over there. What can they be gathered there for?" She pointed to a group of people standing beside the long pier. They were clustered around a bracken-covered form stretched out on the sand. The group was bickering amongst themselves – the men's voices raised in anger. One of them reached down and turned the lump over. It was clearly quite heavy. Two gulls circled overhead, very interested in that section of the beach.

Althea had a sudden sickening feeling in the pit of her stomach. She looked around. The group behind them were still engaged in conversation and the rest of the party some ways ahead were also. She said with feigned lightness, "Why don't you stay here, dear Jane. Perhaps His Grace will be so kind as to come with me in order to investigate." And then she set off at a brisk pace before Norwich could stop her, striding across the expanse of sand towards the group.

Norwich grabbed her arm as he caught up to her, "Now see here, Althea —"

She gave him a sharp look. "It is a dead body. I would know the human form anywhere. Please don't make a scene. It will be unpleasant enough as it is when our party notices what is going on."

"Surely this poor unfortunate isn't a concern of yours," and then, when it was clear she was going whether he liked it or not, "I'm coming with you."

The group around the body consisted of three scruffy older men, a young laborer with a long-handled shovel draped casually over his shoulder, and a blousy young woman with an indecently low-cut bodice. The men noticed Norwich first and immediately stopped the argument. They regarded him with a measure of respect and hostility.

The young lady, who had her back to Althea and Norwich, continued on, "I think it is that fine tall gentleman what was staying in the Blue Bottle not three nights ago."

"And how would you know anything about a fine tall gentleman at the Blue Bottle?" the young man said suspiciously.

"Leave off your ideas, Joe. Big Meg over at the Blue Bottle told me what they had a gentleman staying with a blue coat and silver buttons. He done and lost one and Meg found it back behind the bar, see, which made her think just what sort of trouble a bloke like that could have done back behind the bar."

The young man hardly seemed mollified but was cut off from reply by Norwich saying in his imposing voice, "Just what do we have here?"

One of the older men kicked at the brown lump. "'Tis a gift of the sea, Governor. Bill here," he stuck a thumb out in the direction of another man with a dirty cap, wet shirt and stained breeches, "found him down around a post of the pier here and drug him out. We was just arguing about what to do with him."

"I'm sure you were. Well, I'll tell you what to do. One of you can run off and find the magistrate." He turned to Bill. "You there, look lively and go find him. There's a coin in it for you if you are quick about it."

The man shuffled off in what might charitably be considered a trot. Althea crouched down and took a good look at the corpse. The body had been turned face up. It was significantly more bloated than the baron had been, making Althea think that he must have gone into the water several days before. The face would be difficult to identify because the skin was beginning to peel away, but even though the clothing was covered with a layer of silt and plant matter, it remained intact. The blue coat was a soggy blackish gray, but the silver buttons seemed good as new.

Norwich forced the other people to stand back from the body and was soon joined by Verlyn.

"I told the rest of the party to go on to the inn without us. So is this what it looks like?" Verlyn said.

Norwich nodded. "Yes. These fine people found him under the pier and hauled him out."

Althea noticed that Norwich took pains to avoid looking at the corpse, but Verlyn apparently had a stronger stomach because he crouched down beside Althea. "Do you think he drowned?"

"Perhaps afterwards. A bullet got him first." She pointed to a section of the head just behind the ear. The hair was gone and the skull dented inwards. "The bullet is likely still in the brain because I don't see an exit wound on the face. A small gun. Perhaps even a lady's pistol."

Verlyn nodded. "Do we have any sense of who he might be?"

The young lady crouched down beside them and gave Verlyn an engaging smile. "He was a fine gentleman what stayed at the Blue Bottle Inn. Big Meg would know what name he signed in the books."

"Where is this Blue Bottle Inn?" Verlyn said.

"On Chambers Street. I can show you, sir, if you would like me to."

"That'll do, Bonnie. You got chores to do and all," the young man said.

Verlyn nodded. "Yes, I wouldn't want you to waste time on me. I'm sure I can find the place if I need to. Thank you."

Bonnie blushed up to the roots of her hair and would have stayed at Verlyn's side if Joe hadn't pulled her up by the arm. "We'd best be getting home."

She went reluctantly and called over her shoulder, "Big Meg at the Blue Bottle."

Norwich chuckled. "You have an admirer, brother."

Verlyn grinned and then, looking back at the corpse, his face went white. "Wait, I know him. It's James Nettles." He stood up abruptly and turned away. "Oh my God."

Althea stood up as well. "How do you know?" she said in a low voice so that the scruffy pair still left couldn't hear her.

Verlyn ran a hand over his face. "The signet ring. He used it to sign his letters. I have to get word to London."

Norwich turned back towards the two stragglers. "Move along now. No more to see here."

They seemed reluctant to leave – likely thinking that there might yet be an opportunity to plunder the body or to wheedle some money out of two fine gentlemen – but Norwich's stern gaze and commanding presence eventually made them think better of that. They wandered back up the beach.

When they were out of earshot, Norwich said, "Was Nettles employed by the government?"

Verlyn nodded. "He was one of the men who acted the part of the Richmond Thief."

Althea said, "I think we should come to an agreement as to what we are to tell our party. My thought would be to say it appears that this unfortunate man must have imbibed too heavily and managed to fall off the pier and drown himself. I doubt those two gentlemen just leaving us will be in a position to contradict us with our own party."

Norwood nodded. "The magistrate should be told. However, I doubt he will have the wherewithal to solve a crime involving his majesty's agents."

"I shall ask the magistrate to hold the body until James' family can claim it," Verlyn said.

They fell silent for several minutes, each lost in his or her own personal thoughts. Then Althea looked up and spied a well-dressed man coming towards them. He was accompanied by several men in naval uniforms, with the disreputable Bill trotting behind. "I think that this must be what we are waiting for," Althea said.

Norwich turned to Verlyn. "Why don't you take Lady Trent back to our party? It is better that you not be seen to be involved. I can take care of this."

Verlyn clapped his hand on Norwich's shoulder. "You are the best brother." Then he extended his arm. "Come, Lady Trent."

She took his arm and turned back towards the town. As she did, something tickled the back of her memory. The half-moon of the harbor with the streets winding their way up through the hills reminded her of something. But what was it? It took the entire trip across the sand until she had it. "Lord George! The piece of paper we found on the baron. It is a map – a map of Torquay."

"Torquay?"

"Yes. The lines represent the shoreline of the harbor and the roads leading away from the harbor."

He disengaged her arm and pulled out his watch. Extracting the paper carefully so that it wouldn't blow way, he held it up.

"See, there is the shore and those are the roads. But here, where that line ends, there appears to be a small *x*. I hadn't noticed that before. Perhaps something is hidden at that point?"

"It could be!" He tucked the paper back in the watch. His whole demeanor had shifted and his eyes shown bright, like a child given a new toy. "Althea, you are a wonder!" He impulsively grabbed her hand and kissed it. "I shall tell Sir Neville that I have been called back to London and then come here to investigate." He took another two steps. "But we still do not know what *Al Andalus* means, unless you have a theory?"

"I am afraid not at the moment."

They continued on until they met the rest of the group at the Pelican Inn. The Pelican was a well-kept inn with several private rooms on the ground floor. Sir Neville had reserved the largest for the Ranleigh party, and the long table was full to bursting with cold meats, breads, pickles, jellies, aspics and every good thing for a substantial luncheon.

There was much furor and conversation about the body on the beach as soon as they entered the room. The ladies had much to say on the subject of their shock and disgust. Mr. Smithson also seemed as hysterical as the women in decrying the horror of the moment. "I dare swear I have never seen such a thing. It made me feel quite faint. Fortunately, Mrs. Gregson was swift in the production of her smelling salts. If she hadn't been forward-thinking in bringing them in her reticule, I don't know where we might have been," he said to Althea, when she was finally able to take her seat.

"I agree that it is most distressing, but His Grace has taken it upon himself to wait with the poor unfortunate man until the magistrate can assume control of the situation. Living on the edge of the ocean as he does, the magistrate must have developed a certain skill in handling the drowned, particularly now that the Navy has made such use of the harbor. Unfortunately, our naval vessels are not immune to accidents."

"So true, Lady Trent. It is, I'm sure, a sad reality for the magistrate. I certainly do not envy him." Mr. Smithson shuddered dramatically. And then, seeming to recover his composure, he said, "But is it certain that this death was an accidental drowning?"

"A drowning, yes," she said with firmness, "but I cannot speculate as to its accidental nature or not. I suppose someone could have pushed the man overboard, but I think it highly unlikely."

"So he was a sailor then?"

"Oh no. I'm sorry if I gave that impression. He was a civilian by his clothes. I am just assuming that with an accidental drowning, one would most likely fall off a boat." Althea felt the time had come for evasive measures. "I wish I knew more, but it is still so very distressing, Mr. Smithson."

"So sorry, Lady Trent. I'm afraid that my curiosity is morbid, but it is all so very terrible. My nerves have suffered a severe shock, I have no hesitation in telling you. I don't know how you can take things as calmly as you always seem to do. It is as if corpses are second nature to you."

Althea smiled self-consciously. "Well, I suppose they are. I assisted my husband with his research into *Dermestes trentatus*, a peculiar beetle that feeds on decaying flesh, and my father was a renowned physician. Death is second nature in those circumstances."

"I had heard some gossip about a scientific paper of some sort. A Trent Method, I believe? Was that your husband's work?"

Althea swallowed hard. It still rankled that she had to use her dead husband's name in order to have her own work published. "Yes. It is a method to determine how long a body has been buried by examining the types and development of the insects found on the corpse. I have been told that it represents quite a breakthrough for criminal detection."

"Oh, well that is just too bad, isn't it?"

"What is?"

"That this body was found at sea. Unless you know of some method there?"

"No, unfortunately not."

Mr. Smithson smiled and shook his head. "If you had, that would be quite the thing. Can you imagine the poor magistrate with all of his experience being told his business by a lady of refinement? It would be so terribly droll."

Althea wasn't sure whether to be offended or pleased with that statement, and so she gave him a thin smile in return.

Norwich returned within the hour, and after a substantial repast, the party decided to avoid the shoreline for a walk in the streets of Torquay. They were just about to depart when Lady Batterslea, who had been idly staring out a window, suddenly exclaimed, "I dare swear it is Lord Tunwell! I wonder what he is doing here?"

"I'm sure you are mistaken, my dear," Lord Batterslea said dismissively. "The man's at Tunwell Court dealing with his uncle's affairs."

"I think I should know the new baron after dining with him as we have. I tell you, it is him. Come see, if you don't believe me."

Lord Batterslea made his way to the window. "Where?"

"Over there. Down the street."

"It is merely a fair-haired man with a beaver hat. I don't know how you can say it was him."

"Well, now that his back is to us, he could be confused with anyone, but he turned and looked at me a minute ago."

Lord Batterslea chuckled. "Of course he did, my dear. Come, we are all waiting on you."

The streets of Torquay were narrow and winding and the party moved more slowly than Althea, who was used to long brisk walks, normally tolerated. She had thought to maneuver herself next to Norwich in order to have further conversation with him about the body on the beach and her discovery regarding the scrap of paper, but he seemed to be in a taciturn mood and eluded her attempts to reach him. She finally gave up and dedicated herself to listen with half an ear to Mrs. Gregson, who was engaged in a long and rather tedious story about a friend of hers who had died some years before. The point of the tale seemed to be that one should live one's life in an upright manner and keep honest company.

It was when the party turned and headed back towards the ocean and the street where the carriages had been drawn up, that Althea finally gave up even the pretense of listening to Mrs. Gregson. Instead, she studied the water. The waves were so beautiful as the sunlight touched the tips of their regular peaks. The wind had died down enough that the walk presented no difficulties of dress. Indeed, the day was as fine as any day Althea had yet experienced. If Althea had had any choice in the matter, she might like to live by the ocean and be a daily witness to the wonders of the marine world. She wondered idly if the duke had any coastal properties and then chided herself for being silly.

She turned her mind back to a more serious subject. Mr. Smithson was correct in that there should be equal mechanisms of criminal detection for the sea as on land. Perhaps some intrepid scientist had already identified them. England was a seafaring nation, and so it only stood to reason that some study must have been done. She would write to Mr. Read when they returned to Ranleigh and find out.

And then, she finally remembered something that had been teasing her. Mr. Smithson's waistcoat – the pillars and lions – it was the labors of Hercules. That was the mythological allusion that had eluded her before.

CHAPTER FIFTEEN

The following morning, Althea made her usual perambulation around the gardens of Ranleigh before seeking breakfast. She rambled a little farther that usual, lost
in her own tangle of thoughts. When she returned, only
Lord and Lady Pickney were present in the breakfast room,
finishing a leisurely rasher of bacon and some half a dozen
eggs.

"Well, I suppose you must have known all about it, but
it certainly surprised me when Mrs. Gregson told me this
morning," Lady Pickney said.

Althea poured herself some coffee. "What is that?"

"We are suddenly bereft of our two finest conversation-
alists. Norwich left early this morning, saying he had some
urgent business at Austell Abbey, and Lord George has gone
off to London! I tell you, I shall feel their absence quite
forcefully because, between you and me, they were some of

the few of our fellow guests with a particle of sense about them. Although I suppose that I should be grateful that the Batterslea woman won't be forever fawning over Norwich. I don't know how you could stand to be in the same room with her – not that you need have worried, of course."

Althea took a sip of coffee in order to give her time to steady her nerves. Verlyn she knew about, but Norwich's behavior was a complete and utter surprise. In truth, she didn't know what to make of it. If it had been Bath, it would have indicated that his mother had taken a bad turn, although he surely would have extracted an answer from her if that had been the case. Perhaps he no longer cared to formalize the engagement. She couldn't think about that now.

She decided honesty was the best policy with someone as sharp as Lady Pickney. "I'm afraid I am not in anyone's confidence, and so I have no further knowledge on the subject. I only hope that they have safe travels."

Lady Pickney smiled. "In other words, you dare not tell us."

"My dear, I'm sure Lady Trent has a right to be believed when she speaks," Lord Pickney said good-naturedly.

"Do not worry, my lord, Lady Trent and I understand each other very well. There was no harm meant."

"None taken," Althea replied. "Are you fully rested from yesterday's adventure?"

"I feel much better than I did last night at supper, I can certainly tell you. No matter how well sprung a carriage is, I always feel the effect of being tossed about down deep in my bones. I suppose age must account for it because I don't ever remember having to curtail a journey when I was young for such a silly reason. It puts me all out of patience with myself."

Althea smiled. "You must forgive your poor bones as they are the only ones you have and so should be treated with some care."

"And how did you like Torquay, Lady Trent? Had you been there before?" Lord Pickney said.

"No, never, but I found the place as delightful as any place I have ever visited. There is something so invigorating about the sea air."

"I quite agree," he answered, "despite the unfortunate incident on the beach. But then, I suppose that drownings must occur even in the best locations. Did the magistrate have any idea who the man was?"

"I do not know. I left with Lord George as the magistrate was just coming up the shore."

Lord Pickney shook his head. "It is certainly a sad business. I am so glad that it has not colored your view of Torquay, however. Despite my lovely wife's bones, I had thought to mention another excursion there, if others in the party feel as you do."

"I think that is a wonderful idea, and I will certainly join you, if I may."

Later that afternoon, when she was just about to walk in the rose garden with Jane, Althea received a letter from London. She thought perhaps it might be Norwich for a fleeting moment, but realized from the direction scribbled on the front and the various pen stains that it must be from Magistrate James Read of Bow Street.

"And what does the magistrate want with you now?" Jane said. Jane knew all about Althea's work with the Bow Street

Runners but maintained skepticism about the wisdom of incurring dangerous risks for the pleasure of helping the court.

Althea tucked the letter into her reticule and then proceeded to unfurl her parasol. "I have some new ideas for investigative processes and sought Mr. Read's guidance."

"Oh, is that all? I thought for sure that you had written him about the baron's death."

Althea smiled self-consciously. "You are too clever, my dear sister. I did mention Lord Tunwell's passing, of course, but only in the vaguest details."

"And I'm sure he will respond that it was most likely an accident, for really, Althea, what else could it be?"

"Yes, I suppose you are correct. In any case, as it is a fine day, I think I can probably leave off matters of criminal investigation for a couple of hours and enjoy your company. It seems we are always running about and do not have the time to discuss matters properly. How did you like Torquay? For myself, I thought Sir Neville did an admirable job of organizing the expedition and, had it not been for the dead body, the day would have passed off perfectly."

"I liked it very much and will admit that Sir Neville has a knack for that sort of thing. He has been a fine host to us here at Ranleigh."

They reached the garden and Althea paused to admire a particularly fine tea rose with a honeyed smell. Jane did not say more and Althea sensed a tension in her erect form. Althea turned back to her. "You have something to tell me, Jane?"

Jane looked down. "I don't even know how to begin, but I think I shall accept Sir Neville's most obliging offer. He is not perhaps the most dashing figure, but I do think he could make me happy. At least, I have as good a chance as I have with anyone."

"Oh Jane!" Althea hugged her impulsively. "I do wish you the very best in life, and to see you married to a good man and mistress of an estate such as Ranleigh gives me the greatest pleasure in the world!"

Jane pulled away and then dug for a handkerchief in her reticule. "I don't know why I'm suddenly misty-eyed. It is so unlike me." She dabbed her face.

"You are to be a bride! That is reason enough for emotion. Have you gone so far as to set a date?"

Jane chuckled. "First, I have to tell Sir Neville."

"What? The poor man doesn't know he is to be happy?

"I wanted to discuss the matter with you before I told him. Do you think I am too old for marriage?"

"No, of course not. And in any case, you are far younger than your brother was when he married me. The Trent family merely waits for maturity – that is all."

"But do you think - I suppose it is indelicate to even discuss the matter, but it has been preying on my mind because, although Sir Neville has indicated that he has no need for an heir as his cousin is young and healthy, still it is expected —"

Althea patted Jane's arm. "While it is true that younger women may more easily conceive, my father attended several women of more advanced age during their pregnancies. And you have always been so healthy that I do not wonder at your being able to withstand the rigors. In any case, if Sir Neville has no need for an heir, then you may safely trust to providence."

"You always tell me what I want to hear, dear Althea."

"I tell you the truth, as well you know. Now we must have no more delays. Poor Sir Neville must hear the good news!"

Sir Neville was duly informed that he was to be the happiest of men and, after an express was sent to the lawyer named as one of the trustees of Miss Trent's dowry, it was felt, in light of the fact that Jane didn't have a father or brother to give consent, an announcement of the marriage could safely be made to the party at Ranleigh.

The news was greeted with much satisfaction because Sir Neville's attentions could not have been any more marked. Sir Neville received the congratulations with great aplomb, and when the talk ran to a request for further details, he added that, "He was ready to be married today if a special license could be procured, but would defer to his dearest Jane's wishes."

Jane smiled and said that she had not given the matter much thought, but would certainly put her mind to it forthwith.

The impending marriage formed the chief topic of conversation for the rest of the day, pushing any discussion of the absence of the Norwich family firmly away. It was only after dinner when the ladies were partaking of tea and coffee that Lady Pickney sidled up to Althea and said in a low voice, "And so you have no further insight into the absence of our distinguished guests?"

"I am afraid that their explanations must suffice because I have no further information."

"I suppose it must be secret, then, if you dare not tell it."

"I have no special information, I promise you. They have urgent business and that is all. It is to be hoped that they will rejoin us when the business is completed."

Lady Pickney sighed. "Well, it is a great thing for Sir Neville and Miss Trent, but I had assumed another marriage might also be in preparation. The duke's sudden appearance here would seem to have confirmed it, but I suppose that these things take time."

Althea nodded her head in a noncommittal sort of way and then changed the subject, hopeful that only Lady Pickney would have the audacity to question her about Norwich.

It wasn't until she had prepared for bed that she finally had a moment to read the letter from Mr. Read. It was a long letter, full of information about a ring of female pickpockets recently apprehended who had been preying on wealthy women at society functions, and interest in her theory regarding soil. He was so encouraging about her hypothesis that she began to hope that the work might just make another monograph for the *Philosophical Transactions* – assuming the result could be proved, of course. She would have to develop a scale for description, as well to differentiate the characteristics, and that would take time.

She retired to bed, her head full of soil and beetles and the piercing look of an absent duke.

CHAPTER SIXTEEN

A lthea had to admit that the duke's sudden departure unnerved her. She hoped that he would send a note of explanation, but as the days passed and no note came, she began to wonder if her insistence on time had irrevocably sent him away.

No matter, she told herself, *I have a son and a home and dear Jane to comfort me.* However, dear Jane seemed more and more occupied with Ranleigh. It was only natural, as Jane was soon to be its mistress. Althea could feel the first crack of what she was sure would be a larger chasm dividing them from each other, as time and distance and interests diverged. Ever since Althea had gone to Dettamoor Park as a new bride, Jane had been there as a friend and confidante and a true and devoted sister. Althea could hardly begrudge Jane the new title of Lady of the Manor at Ranleigh.

As a distraction from the melancholy of her thoughts, Althea increased the frequency of her rambles across the grounds and could be found, if anyone desired to find her, engrossed in producing a series of fine sketches of the pond life, both plant and animal. In this occupation, she was discovered one afternoon by Mr. Ogden, who had been sent to plant rushes on the far side of the pond. He would have passed on, but Althea, tired of her own company, sought to engage him once more regarding the construction of the pond.

"It has often been my observation that good soil may be followed by bad in layers downward. Did you not encounter such layers as you dug?" she said.

"Not as you would say bad soil, Lady Trent, for the Ranleigh land has always been fine, but yes, we met with a variety of soils as we dug. Several layers of rich dark soil was hauled away for use in the hot house and for the roses."

"And did you find anything unusual? Buried treasure, so to speak?"

He chuckled. "An axe head and some bits of iron that didn't seem to belong to anything was all the treasure we found."

"And once you had excavated this spot, how did you manage to fill it with water?"

"Aye, that was the easiest part. It rains something fierce in the spring and fall. We had only to wait for the good Lord to give us a couple days of showers and the thing was nearly done. We diverted the course of one part of the stream temporarily for the rest."

"Of course. I am a simpleton. Once you had the water, the animals will soon follow, although I assume you stocked the fish?"

"Yes, Lady Trent, and planted the reeds and so forth. Sir Neville was most particular about all of it. He had this gentleman who designs gardens out to see the progress several times in order to make sure it was just as he wanted."

"Well, it is a lovely pond, so I don't wonder that it took a great deal of planning. I am sorry to have kept you so long, Mr. Ogden."

Althea watched him walk away, her mind turning over and over everything she knew. It just didn't make sense. She packed up her charcoals and drawing paper and began the walk back to the house. She was within sight of it when a movement out of the corner of her eye caught her attention. A man on horseback was galloping away from the house, down the long drive, toward the road. He was a small man, by the look of it, on a very fast black horse. It took her a moment before she comprehended. That must be Mr. Smithson. But where was he going in such a hurry?

On impulse, Althea hurried up to her room. "Miss Dorkins, I need my riding habit. I feel like riding for a bit."

A servant had conveyed her request that the pony be saddled, and so, when Althea arrived, he was ready to mount. Instead of mounting him, however, Althea engaged an older groom in idle conversation.

"Andalusia is such a funny name for a common pony. I was told that he had been owned by a Spanish gentleman, but can't imagine a Spanish gentleman living in the vicinity."

"He came from Torquay," the groom replied, as if that explained everything.

"Are there many Spanish gentlemen in Torquay?"

"Can't say, what with the war and all – many sorts of strange folks come to live there."

"Yes, that makes sense. Do you have family in Torquay?"

The groom nodded, clearly uncomfortable speaking with a lady about anything so personal. "Yes, madam."

"I thought it a lovely place to live. The ocean has such a wonderful sound to it, don't you think?"

He nodded again. "Yes madam. My cousin says the harbor is as fine as any in England. They get the finest ships in the Navy come to port."

"I can certainly believe it. It must be lovely to have such a place within a couple of hours' distance."

The groom smiled.

"Have I said something amusing?" Althea said in an encouraging way.

"No, madam, it's just that it wouldn't take more than an hour if you were to ride a good horse and know the way."

"I see. Sir Neville was obviously thinking of our comfort when he decided to take the main roads. I suppose a carriage would not traverse some of the paths you suggest?"

"No madam."

"So any of the guests here at Ranleigh might easily go there and back in a morning?"

"Very easily, madam. Why that Mr. Smithson, with the fine black horse, is forever coming and going."

"How interesting." She then received a brief description of the route to be taken to Torquay and, after asking several more probing questions and committing the whole to memory, said, "I have detained you long enough. I think I will take the path around the west pasture and circle back again."

She climbed up the block and mounted the pony. As she was adjusting her skirts, she wondered how it must feel to ride a horse properly like a man. Perhaps she could make the experiment when she returned to Dettamoor Park with one of Sir Arthur's old saddles. It was entirely possible that the constriction of the saddle was what had always prevented her from enjoying a gallop across the fields.

She completed enough of a circuit to be believable and then returned to the stables. The same groom assisted her down. "Thank you, kind sir. What is your name, by the way, so that I may commend you to Sir Neville?"

He blushed. "Stiles, madam. They call me Stiles."

"Mr. Stiles, thank you again."

When Althea returned to her room, she found Jane changing her dress in preparation to go into the village with Sir Neville. "Dear Jane, what would you say to a long ride tomorrow morning? Or do your new duties preclude time away?"

"I'm sure I can be spared for a morning," Jane replied, with a twinkle in her eye, "but what is this about riding horses? You have never been an avid horsewoman. What are you up to now?"

"Nothing particular, except a trip to Torquay by the back roads. I am informed by a credible source that it takes roughly an hour."

"And why do you wish to go to Torquay?"

"Curiosity. I think that is where Mr. Smithson rides off to so frequently, and I want to know why."

"Mr. Smithson? I expect he goes merely to take the air and then enjoy an ale at the end of it."

"Quite possibly, but there is no harm in seeing for ourselves."

"No, I suppose not. Besides, it will give us time for conversation. I wish to solicit your advice about the wedding."

So, the next morning, the ladies set out together. It was a fine day for a ride and the directions Althea had memorized turned out to be reasonably accurate. In a little over an hour, they were above Torquay looking down at the harbor, exactly, if Althea's memory served her, where the *x* had marked the spot on the map. The harbor was filled with tall ships and little boats of every description, and they could see sailors clambering about the pier and walking the beach.

"They must be preparing to go to sea," Jane said.

"I think you are correct. Let us only hope that Mr. Bonaparte is not as well equipped."

"I have faith in the Navy. Father always said England was nothing but for her navy. It is a great deal too bad that we no longer can boast of Nelson, poor man, but I'm sure our current command has the affair well in hand."

"Let us ride down into the town and see for ourselves, shall we? And then perhaps some refreshment at one of the inns. All of this riding has left me parched," Althea said.

The path down towards the town was narrow and winding and delayed them another twenty minutes, but then they were in the streets of Torquay. As they had seen from above, the town was full of persons going to and fro, attending to the naval personnel down at the harbor. The ladies meandered in and out of the narrow streets until Althea found what she was looking for. "I think we will inquire about a parlor here," she said, as she reined her horse in at the yard of the Blue Bottle Inn.

An ostler approached them and helped them to alight. Upon admittance to the parlor, they were informed that a private room was available for a light luncheon.

When they were left alone, Jane said, "Now tell me why we have come here. It cannot be to follow Mr. Smithson, for we have seen nothing of the man."

"That was only part of the reason, although this trip has proved to me that one may easily travel back and forth to Torquay from Ranleigh. I wanted to come to the Blue Bottle because I was told that the body we found on the beach had stayed here before his untimely end."

"You don't think it was anything but an accident, do you?" Jane said.

A servant entered with two glasses of claret on a tray and a second followed with a small selection of bread, pickles and cold meats. Once the food was laid out and the servants had retired, Althea said, "No, but still I wondered what sort of inn it might be. And as this one seems most respectable, I suppose he couldn't have been involved with anything very nefarious. Probably just a little too much to drink and a wobbly walk along the pier."

Jane nodded, apparently satisfied. "This beef is very good, by the way."

Althea tried a piece. "It is indeed. So now that my curiosity has been fed, tell me more about your plans for the wedding. Does Cousin John know we are to hold it during his visit to Dettamoor Park?"

"I have written him, and he tells me he is most happy to come and stand with me."

They talked on about the wedding plans while Althea tried to figure out how she might speak to the woman known as Big Meg without arousing Jane's suspicions. In any case, the opportunity presented itself more easily than Althea could have imagined.

A large woman appeared with two more glasses of claret and asked if the ladies needed anything further. Jane inquired after the facilities and Althea made some pretext about discussing the preparation of the beef, so that once Jane had left the room, Althea said, "Sorry to be impertinent, but I don't have much time. You are called Big Meg, are you not?"

The lady looked surprised. "Yes, madam."

"A friend of yours named Bonnie found a dead gentleman on the shore. She said the man had stayed at this inn prior to his death and that you would know something about him. Do you remember a tall gentleman in a blue coat with silver buttons?"

"Aye, I do, but as I told the magistrate at the time, I don't know much about him. He called himself Cartwright and said he was a banker from London."

"Did he say what his business was or if he was meeting someone?"

"No, madam, nothing like that. He just said he was here for business. I didn't ask for details, it not being my place and all."

"I understand, but can you think of anything he did or said that was unusual? Even the smallest detail may be helpful."

"And begging your pardon, but why do you want to know?"

"It was the cousin of the lady I am traveling with. His death was so sudden and so shocking that she wants to know anything that may give her a fuller understanding. But the subject is too painful, you understand, for her to ask these questions herself. I am merely trying to assist her as her friend."

Meg nodded with understanding. "I can see how that might be. He was a kind gentleman, I can tell you that. Nothing high and mighty about him. One thing, though, he didn't seem comfortable like a gentleman usually is. Nervous, I'd say. Like he was looking over his shoulder while he was talking to you. But I suppose a stranger in a new place would be nervous."

"Did he say it was his first time in Torquay?"

Meg thought for a moment and then replied, "No, now that I come to think of it, he said that he was in Torquay last summer because he asked me about some repairs they did to the pier in the autumn."

Althea heard the sound of Jane's footsteps. She pressed a coin into Meg's hand. "Thank you most kindly. Now, not a word to my friend, or we'll have her in tears again."

Meg nodded solemnly and quickly withdrew.

The ride back to Ranleigh seemed longer than the ride to Torquay. Perhaps it was the accumulated fatigue of the journey or the fact that the sun was now full on them, but neither lady was sad to see the turn onto the long drive into the Ranleigh grounds. They urged the horses forward, and the horses, sensing respite and food, trotted along at a sprightly clip. They were met by the sight of a dashing carriage just pulling up to the house.

"I wonder who that can belong to?" Jane said.

"Someone with good taste in carriages."

"And money."

A blond gentleman with a high hat and a dark coat alighted from the equipage. "Why, I believe it is the new baron," said Althea.

"It can't be. Surely his duties to his late uncle preclude him from returning here so quickly?"

"I don't think he cares much for duty. Come, Jane, let's get these horses stabled as quickly as possible so that we may discover the truth of the matter."

CHAPTER SEVENTEEN

Once changed, they made their way down to the rose salon, where Lady Pickney was ensconced in a high back chair ostensibly engaged in some needlework but really partaking of some delicious gossip with Mrs. Gregson. When the ladies entered, she dropped her work to her lap and said, "Ah, just the very ladies I wished to speak to. Have you heard the news? Lord Tunwell has returned to us."

Althea nodded. "We saw him come up the drive as we returned from our ride. I had thought that he meant to stay at Tunwell Court."

"So did we all," said Mrs. Gregson, "but apparently he prefers our society to the society of Tunwell Court."

"But surely the mourning rigors have not lessened yet?" said Jane.

Lady Pickney clicked her tongue. "He wears a black band on his hat. I suppose that that is all that is required in this day and age."

"He is a wicked, ungrateful young man," said Mrs. Gregson.

"One can only hope that his sudden elevation will have caused him to think more highly of his position in society. He has the obligations of the title now," Althea said.

"If you think money will turn him respectable, I will think you very naïve, Lady Trent," Mrs. Gregson said.

"Not naive, I assure you. I merely mean that he now has a great deal to lose, which he didn't before."

Mrs. Gregson seemed about to argue, and so Lady Pickney said, "And you and Miss Trent went for a ride this morning – was it pleasant?"

"Very much so. Jane and I are becoming quite accustomed to the countryside here about, which is a very good thing for the future Lady Tabard."

This remark led inevitably to a discussion of the wedding, which occupied the next full hour, and soon thereafter all of the ladies retired to their rooms to prepare for a simple dinner. Dinner was completed without much ceremony and the party took the opportunity to rest, or, in Althea's case, to read a book from Sir Neville's library before the evening's festivities.

Sir Neville had invited a well-known singer on tour throughout England to come and perform a musical concert for his guests and select neighbors. Extra care was taken by all in the manner of dress so as not to shame their host. Althea chose the yellow dress Norwich had commented upon and did her hair with some golden roses cut from Ranleigh's gardens.

She was the first to arrive to the large drawing room at the back of the house. The room had been set up with a collection of chairs towards the door and five chairs facing the audience to accommodate a quintet hired to accompany Signora Campobello. They sat tuning their instruments. Althea settled into a chair and slowly fanned herself with a silk and ivory fan decorated with a classical scene that Lady Bertlesmon, Norwich's sister, had given her during their brief sojourn at Norwich House. She had to admit that her spirits sunk whenever she thought of anything having to do with the Norwich family, and she would have been glad to have had a word from him.

"Lady Trent, how delightful to see you again."

Althea turned around and beheld Cruikshank in all of his angelic glory. He was dressed with exquisite care in a new evening ensemble, a black armband the only sign of his mourning state. He executed a low bow, with a hint of mockery playing about his mouth. Althea had to admit to herself yet again that he was the most handsome man she had ever beheld.

She stood and extended her hand. "Lord Tunwell. Let me say again how sorry I am about your loss."

He took her hand and kissed it, lingering longer than was seemly. "Come now. We know each other better than that. Tunwell Court was as dull as I had remembered, so I thought I could do nothing better than come back to all my friends at Ranleigh."

Althea smiled. "I think you take great delight in poking fun at us, but for my part, I am glad you have come. You will enliven our little party."

"I had heard that the duke and his brother have abandoned the house. You must be bereft."

"You mistake the matter, sir. I merely meant that any enlargement of our group will be agreeable. Ah, and here we have Sir Neville to begin the festivities."

Sir Neville was resplendent in satin knee breeches and a tight fitting frock coat. He had laced himself up more tightly than usual and his corset gave him the look of a proud bird. He clapped his hands together and the fobs on his watch chain jangled happily. "It is a rare treat we have in store for us. The Signora is just now warming up her voice. She is an artist among artists."

"Thank you again for securing her for us. I had heard tell of her marvelous voice but had not thought I would have such an opportunity. What is to be her program this evening?"

"Italian love songs. I thought it a fitting tribute to my dear Miss Trent."

Althea smiled. "I am sure it will be most fitting. If only other men were as romantic as you, we women would have nothing to complain of."

Some neighbors of Sir Neville were then announced, and so he left Althea to greet them. Jane arrived next and then the Gregsons. When the party was complete, the guests were invited to sit and Althea ended up next to Jane and Sir Neville. Unfortunately, Cruikshank quickly took the seat to her other side before she could object.

"You will have to help me with the Italian translation," he said, "for I have no head for languages."

"And what makes you think I do?" she replied.

"Oh, I have it on good authority that you are a veritable Tower of Babel."

"Well, I have a little Italian," she admitted.

He laughed. "You see, I have the right of it."

Althea hushed him at that moment because Signora Campobello arrived. She was a small lady with a head of thick dark hair and a regal bearing. Althea could not help but admire the way she immediately took control of the room, all eyes focused on her every move. She approached the musicians and Sir Neville stood. He gave a short speech expressing his delight with her presence and announcing, as if the assembled guests didn't already know it, that he was to be the happiest of men with his dear Miss Trent. La Signora nodded as if approving his words, and then turned back to the musicians with some whispered instructions.

Finally, they began with the first notes of *Lasciatemi morire* from *Il lamento d'Arianna*. Althea, who had seen a production of the lament during her brief sojourn in London, was transfixed by the Signora's powerful and yet delicate treatment of the first lines, "Let me die, let me die."

Signora Campobello became the sad Ariadne, betrayed by Theseus and unwilling to let Bacchus comfort her in her despair. Althea felt a searing pain in her chest, as if a knife had been struck through her heart. The pain felt so intense that she leaned forward in her chair. *What had come over her?* She looked down, half expecting to see blood pouring from her chest, but there was nothing to explain the pain. Then she experienced a moment of blinding clarity. It was the song! Althea was the lost Ariadne, abandoned by the man she loved. *There. She had admitted the truth to herself and could not take it back.* She loved the Duke of Norwich and she had let him go. No, worse than that, she had thrust him away from her.

She waved her fan in front of her face rapidly, fearing the tears that now stood on the ends of her lashes would roll conspicuously down her cheeks. She had been so foolish to think she could treat love like just another experiment. So foolish to think that any man would willingly wait upon her caprice. He had left without so much as a word between them. She felt Ariadne's crushing despair at having been so betrayed. It was too much.

The song ended and the room erupted in applause. Althea stood up and hurried to the door. She reached the hall and paused for a moment, searching for a handkerchief in her reticule. She would be herself again if she could just have a moment. She found the handkerchief and dabbed her eyes.

"Here, have mine," a voice said behind her.

She turned around. "Lord Tunwell. I got a little over-heated. The song was so lovely —"

"So he left you, did he?"

"I'm sorry, but I don't know what you mean." Althea declined the proffered handkerchief.

"Norwich. I may not be the most proficient Italian scholar, but I have some recollection of mythology."

"I am better now, thank you." She thrust her handkerchief back in the reticule.

"He is a fool, you know."

"I hardly think —"

Cruikshank gave her a long look. "I may be a rake, but I am not a fool, Lady Trent."

Althea heard Jane's voice calling her. "Let us return to the music," Althea replied.

When they returned, Althea repeated the line about becoming overheated and, as the room was rather warm, this seemed to pass for an explanation of her strange behavior. Signora Campobello continued on with her set, including a haunting rendition of *O Del Mio Dolce Ardor* by Gluck and *Caro Mio Ben* by Giordani. Althea sat fixed in rapt attention, in part because the music was exquisite and in part because she could feel Cruikshank's gaze upon her and did not want to encourage conversation.

When the concert was over, Sir Neville invited all of the guests, including the Signora, into supper. This was on a lavish scale and included a cream soup, fish, beef, pheasant and innumerable side dishes. The addition of the neighborhood worthies varied the seating considerably and Althea was happy to note that the baron was not to be seated next to her.

Some very good wine and a delicious soup helped to dispel some of Althea's melancholy, and so she was in an altogether more sanguine frame of mind when the party finally broke up and she climbed the stairs to her bed chamber. After Miss Dorkins had helped her out of her gown and into a nightdress, Althea fell into bed. Her body felt so fatigued that she could barely move to pull the covers up, but as soon as her head hit the pillow, her mind switched on. A thousand thoughts raced through her brain. She replayed Norwich's every look, every word, every touch, and the feel of his arms around her as he rescued her from certain death at the hands of her cousin.

The pain in her chest had turned into a heavy dull ache that pressed downward until she felt as if it would press the breath out of her lungs. She twitched back the covers and pulled the bed curtains aside to get up, but as she did so, she heard a faint creak, like the hinges of the door grinding together. She froze in place and listened. *Yes, someone was definitely opening her door. But why?*

A surge of misguided hope made her think of Norwich. But surely he would not seek to enter her chamber without at least announcing his presence? The soft flicker of candlelight could be seen around the edges of the door and then the door moved again and a dark figure entered the room. It was covered with a long cloak that had a hood thrown over the head and so Althea could not tell if it was a man or woman. Althea lay back down. The figure turned in her direction and Althea shut her eyes; the better to feign sleep. She heard the figure move across the floor and opened her eyes again. It stood in front of the armoire for a moment and raised the candle high, opening the doors with the other hand. And then the hand was darting in and out of the wardrobe, obviously looking for something. *But what could it be?*

Althea heard the sound of drawers being pulled out and fabric being shifted from side to side. This lasted for several minutes. Then the figure reached down and picked something up, a small bundle, tucking the object into the folds of the cloak. Althea gave a sharp intake of breath and the candle swung in her direction. Althea quickly closed her eyes and sighed as if in the midst of a pleasant dream.

She heard the figure approach and saw the increase in the light behind her closed eyelids as the figure held the candle above her. She willed her mind to relax to give her sleep a greater verisimilitude.

The light receded. The man or woman obviously believed her slumber to be genuine. Althea continued still as if in slumber for the next several minutes, while the hinge of her door opened and then shut softly. When she felt as if the intruder must have gone, she arose from her bed and, lighting a candle, made her way to the armoire. What did the thief take?

She searched the armoire for her jewelry and found the locked case tucked neatly at the back of a drawer. Then she located her reticule and purse. She found her letters still tied with ribbon and all of her gloves and hats and parasols. Her shawls as well remained, as did her dancing slippers. "Miss Dorkins will know," she said to herself, before she blew the candle out and climbed back into bed.

After a fitful sleep, Althea awoke to the sounds of birds outside her window. She listened intently, recognizing some of the call and response. "Perhaps I shall spend the day observing the birds," she thought, before the sudden memory of the upheavals of the day before came flooding back. *What did the night time thief steal? And why?*

Althea returned to the wardrobe. She examined all of her dresses and petticoats and stays. They were disordered but still there. She heard a sound behind her and turned to find Miss Dorkins staring with horror at the armoire. "And what have you done, my lady? Everything is so untidy!"

"It wasn't me, dear Miss Dorkins, I can assure you. Now you mustn't breathe a word of this because I do not yet know what it could mean, but I had a strange visitor last night." Althea explained to Miss Dorkins what she had seen.

"I am shocked beyond anything," Miss Dorkins said. "To think of thieves in a house such as this!"

"Do not be alarmed as yet, because nothing seems to have been taken. Did you perhaps store something in this armoire that I was unaware of?"

"No, I cannot think what they could have taken, but I promise I will conduct a complete inventory. We shall get to the bottom of this!"

"Yes, we shall, but again, I beg of you, please say nothing to anyone, even Jane. The thief does not know I was awake and we must keep him or her in ignorance of that fact while we investigate."

CHAPTER EIGHTEEN

The long-awaited trip to Summit Hill was finally to take place. The hill was a picturesque location for an al fresco party in that it combined beautiful views of the countryside and some rather artistic ruins of a fortress that had once stood on the site, Summit Hill being the highest point for many miles around. Sir Neville was on good terms with Lord Bellingham, the owner of the ruin, who lived in a large modern house some distance away, and the outing promised not only an agreeable luncheon, but also an elegant supper with Lord and Lady Bellingham at Ranleigh later that evening.

After the wagons with the food and other arrangements had been sent on ahead, the party set out on horseback. Althea hung back a little, fearing to frustrate faster riders with her slowness, and so she ended up at the back of the line. This provided her the quiet of her own thoughts and an ample view of the machinations of the various members of the party to avoid riding with Lord Tunwell. One rider was not deterred. Lady Batterslea brought her horse up beside him and stayed in this position for most of the ride. Althea guessed that, in the absence of the duke and his brother, she sought to find some diversion by bringing another male to heel with the flutter of her long eyelashes.

The baron was by no means unwilling to entertain her, and Althea caught snippets of light flirtation and laughter every now and then. Their frivolity merely highlighted the continued lowness of her own spirits. She tried to focus on her numerous blessings, including her dear son. She had been happy on her own, she reminded herself, and could not base her future prospects on the caprice of a man, no matter how compelling. This thought led, of course, to all of the reasons she found him compelling, which sent her right back into melancholy.

She was so absorbed in her own thoughts that she didn't notice the passage of time. When she heard Lady Batterslea say, "Oh Lord Tunwell, how you make me laugh with your absurd talk," Althea looked around her and realized that they were nearly at the hill. She forced herself to concentrate because the hill required some horsemanship in that the path was rather narrow.

When they finally reached the summit, Althea understood why the locals made the effort. The views were spectacular, and the ruins, consisting of part of a tower and a low wall, most interesting and picturesque.

"The fortress was originally built by Henry I on the site of a previous Saxon fortification," said Sir Neville, who had dismounted and was standing beside her.

Lady Batterslea and Lord Tunwell came up behind them, and Sir Neville, ever the host, turned to include them in the conversation.

"I find the ruins of a prior age a great spur to the imagination," said Lady Batterslea, with a tittering laugh.

"And what does your fertile imagination produce, Lady Batterslea?" replied Cruikshank, with a sneer that hinted at something indecent.

She fluttered her eyelashes. "Oh, many things."

Althea exchanged a look with Sir Neville and said, "I am glad I brought my sketchbook along. Which do you think the best angle for viewing? Perhaps nearer to the wall?"

"I did not peg you for an artist, Lady Trent," said Cruikshank.

"I drew many of the sketches that accompanied my husband's work, but they were mostly of plants and insects and small animals. Since coming to Ranleigh, I have been inspired to do more landscapes."

"Oh, you should draw portraits. You could do one of me," said Lady Batterslea.

Althea gave her a thin smile. "But I could hardly do you justice, Lady Batterslea, when I am used to drawing beetles, frogs and all manner of horrid things. Why, I might forget myself and give you spots or, worse yet, antennae."

Cruikshank threw his head back and laughed, but Lady Batterslea made a sour face and sought to move away from them. It seemed as if she expected Cruikshank to follow her, but that gentleman stayed on, complimenting Sir Neville on his extensive preparations. Then Sir Neville left them to assure himself that the wafer-thin ham was being properly handled.

After a pregnant moment, Althea said, "You really shouldn't let Lady Batterslea make you a conquest. She might think you are in earnest."

"You do not mince words, do you, Lady Trent? But I find I like your frank way of speaking. Do not worry. Lady Batterslea may think what she likes, for I cannot imagine a worse fate than being in any way permanently attached to such a creature. Besides, she could do with being crossed in love. Otherwise, she will continue to think too well of herself."

"She is young yet."

"And you are old enough to judge?"

"I am a somber widow, Lord Tunwell."

"Yes, very somber. And so filled with good advice, too."

Althea wasn't sure whether to be offended or not. "I beg your pardon if I have done nothing but lecture you. I'm sure you must find proselytizing to be a great bore."

He smiled. "You do it admirably well. It is a new experience to have everyone suddenly encouraging me to the straight and narrow path. Those that will actually speak to me, that is. Why, even good Sir Neville was kind enough to say that my elevation should assist me to re-enter polite society. What he doesn't perhaps realize is that I do not care much for polite society."

"Then why have you graced us with your presence again?"

He gave her an enigmatic look. "Oh, a great many reasons, I assure you."

Sir Neville called the group to order at that moment and presented Lord and Lady Bellingham, who had just arrived. They were a little older than Sir Neville and appeared to be quite devoted to each other in the way that couples of long-standing demonstrate – a warm look here and a gentle touch on the arm there. Althea had met them briefly at the musical evening, and had been very pleased to find that Jane would have such fine neighbors. Lord Bellingham gave a handsome speech welcoming the Ranleigh party to Summit Hill and providing a brief lesson regarding the history of the site. When he was done, the group sat down to a grand feast spread out under an awning stretched between four stout poles.

Althea, who felt that watching happy couples was not perhaps the best tonic for her nerves, maneuvered so as to sit between Lady Pickney and Mr. Gregson. It was clear that he was not in the mood for much conversation, and so Althea discussed the weather and other innocuous subjects with Lady Pickney until Mr. Gregson had finished with his meal and got up to examine the ruin.

"What a disagreeable man," Lady Pickney said, when he was some distance away. "I don't know how Mrs. Gregson puts up with him."

"I do sometimes wonder how he came to be friends with Sir Neville," replied Althea.

"I have come to understand that he was friends with the late baron and that it was Mrs. Gregson who sought the relationship with Sir Neville – likely to receive an invitation to Ranleigh – and, of course, Mr. Gregson was not to turn away an offer that spared him any number of expenses over the summer months. It is well known that he is quite mean."

"Poor Sir Neville, to be so imposed upon!"

"Miss Trent will do a great deal of good if she can wean Sir Neville from such friendships. He appears, on the whole, too little discerning and far too kind."

Althea nodded in understanding. "Jane is very sharp when it comes to people, and I have no doubt that she will have the proper amount of influence to prevent future issues. Still, I would not have known of Mr. Gregson's penury had you not told me. He and Mrs. Gregson dress in quite a fine style."

"I have no doubt he spends money readily enough when it comes to maintaining his consequence."

After the meal, Althea walked to the fortress and selected the most pleasing angle. She then sat on a small blanket to occupy her time with sketching. It was amazing how the mere act of interpreting an object on paper through the medium of her charcoals could provide such peace to her troubled mind. She concentrated on each rounded stone, one on top of the other, until the image appeared in full glory on her paper.

"You are a far better artist than I had expected," a voice said behind her. The sound made her jump in surprise.

"Thank you," she said to Cruikshank, who was grinning down at her. "I'm not sure what you expected."

"No offense, but sensible ladies are often not the least bit artistic."

"None taken, I suppose. I think you must have a very romantic notion of art."

"Likely I do. We have established that my experience with proper ladies is remarkably small."

"Merely encouraging and then jilting them, from what I've heard."

He laughed. "Perhaps, but a girl likes to be crossed in love sometimes. It gives her the push she needs to make a sensible marriage."

"So, you are claiming to be a force for good?" Althea said incredulously.

"Undoubtedly."

Althea refrained from comment. It was dangerous to talk about being crossed in love. She wasn't sure she could do it without some sign of deeper emotion. Instead, she closed her box of charcoals, gathered her papers and stood up. "I think I shall walk the ruins for a bit."

He took the hint, and allowed her to pass beside him. After seeing her things stowed in a saddlebag, she set off to wander the site. The fortress had been situated on the hill such that the slope they had traversed by horse was the gentle one. When Althea reached the other side, she perceived that the drop was quite steep. She moved towards a rocky outcropping at the edge, caught by the sight of some rather unusual bright green lichens. Lichens were an often-overlooked source of both food and medicine, and Althea's father had done no little research on the subject of their properties.

She bent down to examine the lichen and was just trying to decide if it was a form of *Peltigera* or no, when she felt a push from behind. If she had been standing, she could have withstood it, but bent over as she was, the push set her completely off balance. She catapulted over the edge, hitting her head hard against the packed earth just under the outcropping and rolling uncontrollably towards the bottom.

CHAPTER NINETEEN

She supposed later that a normal woman would have screamed for help, but Althea's mind didn't seem to function along normal channels. The first thought that occurred to her was that she had to stop rolling or she would face even more serious injuries, and, as it had once before, an image of a spider, hanging precariously from the warp and weft of its web popped into her head. It could defy the natural order because of the grip of its eight legs on the silken strings.

Althea tensed her arms and legs, trying to grip the hill and create enough friction to slow her descent. About half way down, her efforts finally paid off and she lay limp and spent against the grasses of the hill. She didn't remember much else until she opened her eyes and found the most beautiful face staring down upon her. The light behind the figure gave his fair locks a golden glow like the ring of a halo. *Perhaps I am gone to heaven,* she thought, and then, gathering her wits, *no, it is Lord Tunwell.*

"She is coming around," he said. "Lady Trent, can you hear me?"

Althea looked at him. "Yes. Where am I?"

"On Summit Hill. You took a fall."

"Oh, I must have slipped," Althea replied, still a little muddled.

Jane pushed the baron aside and forced some of the ladies behind her to stand back and give the patient some air. "Althea dearest, we were so worried. Can you move your arms?"

After demonstrating that she had not, in fact, broken her back or any other bone that she could determine, Jane helped Althea to sit upright and then to stand, albeit with the assistance of Jane's arm. Althea perceived that she was back at the top of the hill and wondered exactly who had managed the clamber down to retrieve her.

Sir Neville was all sweetness and solicitation. "My dear Lady Trent, I would not have had this happen for the world! Are you sure you are recovered enough to stand? For surely we can procure a chair for you from somewhere."

"I am well enough to stand, I think, Sir Neville, although my head does swim some, I will admit. I think perhaps it would be best if I returned to Ranleigh as soon as possible to rest for this evening."

"But surely you are not thinking of supper! No, my sister, you must rest. The Bellinghams will not take offense, I assure you. Here, Sir Neville, perhaps your men can help Lady Trent to mount her horse and one of them may lead it. I will accompany her while you play host to the rest of the party," Jane said.

Sir Neville agreed, but when he announced to the group that the Trent ladies were to return, Cruikshank insisted upon accompanying them in case of further accident. Sir Neville, perhaps doubting Cruikshank's intentions, sent several more of his staff to ride along. The augmented party set out at a slow pace.

Althea was very glad that someone with a stronger head was leading her pony because it was enough to simply maintain her body upright. Although she had said that she had slipped, a further review of her memory indicated that someone had very definitely pushed her forward. *But who? Cui bono?*

She thought of Cruikshank, riding behind her. He was a dangerous man, according to Lord George, but Althea seriously doubted he would have pushed her for the sport of it when he seemed more inclined to flirt with her instead. None of the party could have a reason to hurt her that she knew of. Perhaps the push was tied to Althea's mysterious night visitor.

This tangle of thoughts occupied her mind. Jane made gentle conversation when the path widened enough to accommodate the two horses, and Cruikshank rode quietly behind. Thus, the trip was accomplished without further incident. Cruikshank assisted the servant to pull Althea down from her pony. She had felt strong enough to walk, but then her head began to throb as soon as her feet hit the ground, and she stumbled forward. Cruikshank grabbed her arm and supported her as they made their way into the house.

Two maids were called to assist her as soon as they crossed the threshold. Cruikshank lingered as if to continue to walk with Althea up the stairs, but Jane gave him a firm but polite command to locate some smelling salts, in case Althea should faint in the attempt to return to her room. He disengaged from Althea's arm reluctantly.

When Jane had managed to march the party upstairs and force Althea to take a seat in a chair by the fireplace, she sent one of the girls to find Miss Dorkins and the other to fetch a pitcher of hot water and some coals for the grate.

Once the door was shut, she turned to Althea, "You will be the death of me yet, Althea. What were you doing so close to the edge of the precipice?"

Althea put her head in her hands as it had begun to throb once more. "Lichens," she replied weakly. "There was a bright green one I hadn't seen before. But before you blame me, you must know I was pushed. I wouldn't have fallen otherwise."

"Pushed?"

"Yes, but I don't know by whom."

"Why would anyone want to push you?"

"I don't know." Althea hesitated a moment, unsure whether to tell Jane about her night visitor, but as Miss Dorkins might have slipped and mentioned it, she said, "Perhaps it was related to the person who came into my room."

Jane sat down in the other chair. "I was wondering when you might tell me about that. If you swore Miss Dorkins to secrecy, you might have saved your breath. You know that she cannot keep a secret to save her life."

"I know, but I didn't wish to make you worry about me." She gave Jane a complete description of what had happened and then added, "I still do not know what they were after in my wardrobe."

"And Miss Dorkins could not determine it?"

"No. She is as puzzled as I am." Althea sighed.

Jane put her hand on her arm. "Come dear, let me help you change. You must rest."

There was a discreet knock at the door and Jane jumped up to answer it. "Lord Tunwell, you did not need to bring the smelling salts in yourself. That is most kind of you."

"No trouble at all, Miss Trent. I was only too happy. And how does your patient feel?"

He leaned around the door, but Jane stood firmly in front of him. "A little better, thank you. Some rest would do her good, so I'm afraid I will have to close the door and attend to her." And with that, Jane firmly closed the door in his face.

"You would have made a splendid guardian, dearest Jane," Althea said. "My virtue would have been entirely safe in your hands."

"A most imprudent young man," Jane replied.

"But do you think he is an assassin?"

"He was the one who pushed you?"

"I don't know. Norwich warned me against him, so perhaps. But I fail to see what motive he could have for doing so. He would have nothing to gain from my demise, and I don't think I have done anything to anger him. Quite the contrary. He seems to take my moralizing in good humor."

"Norwich may know things that you or I would not be privy to, but I suspect his warning might have more to do with jealousy that any other motive."

"Perhaps." Althea sighed.

Jane gave her a measuring look. "I have held my tongue because I did not wish to press you, and I'm sure this is not the most opportune moment, but what has happened to the Duke of Norwich? Are you still betrothed to him?"

"Dear Jane, it pains me to say that I do not know. I have not broken our engagement, but as to why he left so suddenly and where he has gone, I have no more than that he told Sir Neville that urgent business at Austell Abbey called him away. He has not written to me and I, out of pride, cannot bring myself to write to him to ask for an explanation. And while I know that as a man of honor he would not cast me aside, I have the greatest apprehension that he means through his continued silence to indicate to me that he no longer cares for me."

"And do you care for him?"

Althea felt tears welling up and blinked them away, resolved not to give in to the stabbing pain in her chest. "It is strange, is it not, that one can desire something so completely when one is definitively deprived of it? I find that I love him, Jane, just at the moment when I am very sure that he has ceased to love me."

Jane rose and took Althea's hands in hers. "My dearest sister, no man who has met you could help to fall in love with you. Trust me when I say that I think it will all turn out right in the end. And if it doesn't, Norwich will only have himself to blame for letting the most wonderful woman in England slip through his fingers."

"Oh Jane, I do love you." Althea began to cry in earnest then, letting herself feel, for the first time in a long time, completely and totally lost.

Jane pulled her up and hugged her tight, allowing Althea to sob onto her shoulder for some time. They were discovered thus by Miss Dorkins, who came flying through the door and stopped short.

"Oh, my dear Lady Trent, I am so sorry! I was down in the kitchen speaking to Mrs. Stedman about her recipe for beef jelly, which I have always found to be quite restorative, when I heard the news. How are you feeling?" After the briefest of pauses, "I can tell you are as green an apple. It's no wonder you need dear Miss Trent to support you to stand."

Althea quickly brushed away the last of the tears with a flick of her fingers. "I had quite a nasty fall and do not feel at all myself, Miss Dorkins. Perhaps you would be so kind as to help me undress and into my nightdress. I think some rest would do me a world of good. Miss Trent says I am not to come down to supper either, so I would appreciate if you could arrange to have a tray of something sent up later?"

"Of course you must not go down to supper, you can barely stand! Miss Trent, do not worry, you can leave everything to me."

Half an hour later, Althea was tucked up into bed with a hot brick at her feet and a cup of tea in her hand. Jane had been sent to her room to rest up for supper. Miss Dorkins was fussing about the wardrobe, putting everything to rights and talking to herself in a low voice the way she always did. She had attempted to press some laudanum on Althea, but as her father's daughter, Althea knew that that an opiate solution was the last thing a patient who had banged her head should imbibe.

As she sipped her tea, Althea imagined her future back at Dettamoor Park. How lonely it would be without Jane to keep her company. And Miss Dorkins was surely going to want to stay to attend Jane at Ranleigh, as she had been attending Jane since before Jane's first season. There might be several others, as well, who would follow Jane to her new home. It would be a comfort for Jane to have those about her who knew her ways and habits.

Althea bit back the urge to cry again. Really, she had become so maudlin all of a sudden. It must be the fall. Her father had seen several cases where head injuries had resulted in significant changes to personality. And what if Norwich never came back? She would have to write to him and call the engagement off. It was the only way to release him. She had half a mind to do it immediately, if only to end this torment of uncertainty, but decided to wait a little more to see if some rational explanation for his strange behavior presented itself.

CHAPTER TWENTY

Althea wasn't sure when she slipped off to sleep, but the next thing she knew, the room was dark and Miss Dorkins was no longer to be seen at the wardrobe. Althea thought she had been dreaming. A strange dream about frogs and rushes. One frog turned into a prince when she kissed it. The frog kiss tasted of salty earth, and when the prince leaned down to kiss her as a prince, it was much the same. And then Althea had been swimming in the pond, but the reeds closed in around her and pulled her down to the bottom to where her feet touched the mud.

She sat up with a start. It was the boots. The thief in the night had taken those strange boots! Miss Dorkins must have tucked them into the wardrobe when she couldn't locate their owner and forgotten about them. That was the only item that did not belong to Althea that could possibly have been there. There had to be a connection between the boots and the push down the hill. It was too much of a coincidence to be unconnected.

Althea thought to pull the bell, but refrained. She wasn't sure of the hour of night, and besides, she would just worry Miss Dorkins to no purpose if she had already retired. Althea slid out from under her covers and lit a candle. With any luck, the house would be quiet enough to search.

She observed rather ruefully that any search of Ranleigh House might have been more agreeable had her fall not rendered every movement an agony of pain. It appeared that every muscle and every bone had been bruised by the tumble, and they all cried out in unison as she fastened her wrapper and grabbed the candle. She gritted her teeth. Now was not a time for quibbles.

Once out in the hall, she realized that it wasn't as late as she had originally thought. She heard voices when she reached the stairs, and assumed that the supper party must still be in full swing. A supper would provide her plenty of time to search the bedrooms along the hall. Of course, that still left the staterooms and several other rooms in the other wing.

The boots were clearly women's boots, and Althea knew from passing Lord and Lady Batterslea in the hallway that they were situated in the rooms beyond Jane's. Althea had a hard time picturing Lady Batterslea as a murderess, but her silly demeanor could simply be a clever act. The door next to Jane's produced a neat modern room with a large damask-draped bed, a writing desk, basin stand and an armoire made of figured oak that looked to have been in the Tabard family for some time.

A quick review of the papers under the blotter of the desk revealed tradesmen's bills for a frilled bonnet and an ivory fan covered in silk. The sums were quite large and Althea suspected, given their location, that these bills had not yet been presented to Lord Batterslea. Sir Arthur had had the fortune and the good humor to pay whatever frivolous thing Althea desired, but Althea knew that many women did not have such a husband or such natural restraint. As she returned the bills to their original location, she noticed a slip of paper folded over twice. She pulled it out and unfolded it. Across one side was written in an unfamiliar hand:

Meet me in the roses after dinner
C

Althea refolded it precisely and placed it just as she had found it. The implication was obvious. Lady Batterslea was carrying on a dalliance with someone in the house and the initial would indicate that the former Mr. Cruikshank was the other party. He was playing with fire there. *Auribus teneo lupum.*

Althea quickly reviewed the clothes in the armoire. The boots were nowhere to be found, even in the deep recesses of the piece. This wasn't necessarily surprising, but it did mean that she would now be forced to go to the other wing of the house where the rooms of the Pickneys and the Gregsons were located. Given her general level of pain, this might be no easy task. Althea took a deep breath and marshaled her courage.

Althea's modest background as the daughter of a working physician had given her a somewhat unusual perspective on the relationship between masters and servants in the upper echelon of English society. Unlike most of the people who inhabited that sphere, Althea understood that servants knew more about the workings of a house than anyone else and could be relied upon to act as hidden eyes and ears.

Therefore, when she passed a maid, whom she had been informed by Miss Dorkins was named Betsey, as she went along towards the other wing, she did not automatically pass by without comment. One couldn't assume that the maid wouldn't know or care about strange behavior in her supposed betters. Instead, Althea stopped and said, "Do you know the time? I had sought to rest but find I cannot sleep and perceive that the hour is not as late as I thought."

"It is just now ten o'clock, milady. Should I find Miss Dorkins? I believe she was last in the kitchen asking for a tray to be sent up for your supper. Begging your pardon, but you do not appear to be well enough to leave your room, Lady Trent."

"I am feeling much better, thank you, Betsey, so there is no need to worry Miss Dorkins. I shall return to my room directly. I just wished to know the hour. Don't let me keep you from your work."

The maid curtsied and moved past her. Althea waited until she was out of sight and then hurried to perform her search before Miss Dorkins arrived with a tray and found her gone. The older wing of Ranleigh House had been refurbished but retained much of the original flavor of the building. Ranleigh had been destroyed by fire soon after the first James of England had ascended the throne, and the original wooden structure had been rebuilt with sturdy stone masonry. The house had undergone further transformation under Sir Neville's benevolent ministrations with the expansion of the new wing, which had doubled the living quarters.

Thus, as Althea traversed the passage, she noticed the subtle shift from Grecian elegance to Jacobean solidity. She made her way quickly, but had to duck into a room with an open door once when she heard a servant coming the other direction. She reached the part of the house where the rooms of the Pickneys and Gregsons were located and only waited to determine who was in which room, when she heard a noise behind her. It sounded like footsteps.

She blew out her candle and flattened herself against the wall, but was clearly too slow because a voice called out to her, "Lady Trent?"

"Lord Tunwell," she murmured, frantically seeking a logical explanation for why she was on the other side of the house. And then she had a moment of inspiration. She put her hand to her head. "Oh dear, where am I?"

"Lady Trent, you are not well, let me help you to your room."

She turned as if just now seeing him. "My lord, I feel so faint." And with that she collapsed dramatically to the floor with feigned insensibility.

"Damn," she heard him say under his breath. And then she felt his arms come under her and her feet leave the ground. She willed her mind not to struggle and remain limp in his arms even when he held her too close. She had once been thus carried by the Duke of Norwich and the difference between the present situation and the now dear memory was painful to contemplate.

Cruikshank started forward, walking quickly. Althea heard him say, "I say, you there, come help me."

Another man responded, "Of course, milord. Shall I take her from you?"

"No man, just hold your candle in front of me. She is not well and has become confused."

They continued on until they must have reached her chamber. Althea heard the door creak open and then the cold softness of her counterpane. She remained limp and unmoving while Cruikshank sent the servant away. She resolved to end the charade if Cruikshank attempted anything untoward.

Suddenly, another door opened and Althea heard Miss Dorkin's strident tones. "Oh my lord, what has happened? Why are you here in Lady Trent's chamber?"

Cruikshank sputtered in the face of Miss Dorkin's righteous indignation. "I mean no harm, I assure you! I found Lady Trent wandering on the other side of the house. I have been feeling unwell since this afternoon and left the supper early to go to my rooms. She was out in the hall and then collapsed into insensibility, as you see."

"Dear Lady Trent! How dreadful!" Althea felt her hand jerked upwards and chafed between Miss Dorkin's own. "I won't trouble you any further, Lord Tunwell. Leave everything to me."

When the door closed behind him, Althea opened her eyes. "Thank you, dear Miss Dorkins. I am feeling better already."

"Oh Lady Trent, you gave me such a scare! What were you doing out of your bed?"

"I sought some air, but was found out by Lord Tunwell. I thought a fainting fit might disabuse him of any improper motives engendered by encountering me in my wrapper out in the hall. Did you perhaps secure a tray for my supper? I will admit that I am feeling quite peckish after so much excitement."

Miss Dorkins gave her a wag of her finger. "I am sure I don't know what to do with you. I was so worried when I returned to the room and found you gone. I was just about to raise a search party when Lord Tunwell appeared."

Althea smiled. "I am a trial to you all, I know. And supper?"

Miss Dorkins chuckled. "Never fear, it will be up directly. But you really must rest now. Back under the counterpane, there you go." She tucked Althea in and fluffed her pillow.

"Thank you, Miss Dorkins. I promise I shall stay in bed as you direct from now on."

The next morning, Althea thought it prudent to stay in bed and plead infirmity. This did not fool Jane, however, who came into her room after breakfast.

"You must stop this strange behavior before rumors of madness are spread about you."

"I hit my head, Jane. Any strangeness of behavior must be attributable to that, don't you think?"

Jane looked at her skeptically. "And just what did you hope to learn in the other wing of the house?"

"I was in search of a pair of boots, if you must know. It suddenly occurred to me last night that the only thing that could have been stolen from my wardrobe was something that wasn't mine, namely the boots that Miss Dorkins found."

"Why would someone come and take them back if they did not have the wherewithal to seek them out originally?"

"I do not know, but I feel that that answer will be forthcoming if I can locate who took them from my room."

"And did you find them?"

"No, but I was only able to review Lady Batterslea's room."

Jane sighed. "You must have more care. I know that it was entirely innocent, but having Lord Tunwell carrying you the length of the house is not going to assist your reputation in society."

"So that is already about, is it? I couldn't actually stop him, you know, when I was pretending to have fainted. It would look even more odd."

"I understand, but you would do well to stay in your room today. It will make your behavior seem more of a product of injury."

"Have no fear, dear Jane. I will stay here a week if it makes you feel better. In any case, I am in more pain today than I was before – my father always warned that the second day after injury is worse than the first."

"I'm sorry, I should have asked how you were feeling, I suppose."

Althea laughed. "No, no. You were right to scold me first. What shall I do when you are married away from me?"

Jane sat down on the bed. "I'm sure you will suffer mightily from the lack of my guidance."

CHAPTER TWENTY-ONE

Althea stayed in her room for most of the week. It was not pain that kept her confined, but rather, once she began to draft a monograph, she had trouble focusing on anything else. *Ex nihilo nihil fit.* She had all of her soil samples lined up in a row and meticulously went through them. In all her years of assisting Sir Arthur with the management of the farm, she had never come across a systematic classification of soil, apart from the usual epithets of a soil being *rich* or *sandy* or *full of clay*. One probably existed, but as her purpose was very different, she decided to start afresh and determined to classify her packets by color, mineral content and vegetation. This produced several distinct categories, and she was able by this method to stratify her results in such a way that made certain conclusions grossly obvious.

Thus, by the end of the week, she had her manuscript well enough in hand to write to Mr. Read with a synopsis of her findings and to pen a missive to Lord Aldridge informing him that a new manuscript from the files of the late Sir Arthur would be forthcoming.

Her first trip down to breakfast was not met with any fanfare as she was the only person in the breakfast room. Her early morning habits were not aligned with any other member of the party and so, after breakfast, she took a refreshing turn in the rose garden. The dew sparkled like diamonds on the delicate rose petals. She stroked the downy surface of a large cabbage rose and felt the water drip from her finger. There was no more perfect flower than the rose, she decided. No flower so perfectly combined innocent beauty with decadent fragrance.

It was no wonder that the rose was so universally entwined with the concept of earthly love. Unfortunately, this observation led to thoughts of when she had last been in the rose garden with the duke. She bit her lip so as to stop the flow of tears that bubbled up and threatened to streak down her cheek. She probably would have cried in earnest had Mr. Smithson not joined her.

"I am so glad to see you well again, Lady Trent. It is a fine morning, is it not?"

"Thank you. I did not suspect that you shared my enjoyment of the morning, Mr. Smithson. I did not see you when I breakfasted," Althea replied.

"I am afraid I could not sleep, Lady Trent. A sad malady that I am often afflicted with. I thought I would take a turn in the roses until one of the others came down. Eating breakfast alone is so depressing." He gave a graceful shudder.

"I find I can cheerfully withstand the solitude if the food is well prepared and the coffee hot. It is too bad you suffer so with insomnia." She paused and then casually added, "I have heard that healthful exercise may offer some cure, but then I believe you often ride. Does it help?"

Mr. Smithson did not seem to be bothered by her allusion to his morning rambles, but instead said, "Yes, I find riding to be one of the few delights of the country. Otherwise, the town is much pleasanter, do you not think?"

"I like them both, but am most comfortable in the country."

"Ah, comfort, yes, I suppose it is more comfortable to have a house like this, with grounds and all, even though the society is unvarying and so inevitably dull."

Althea chuckled. "That is why one has an estate of this kind, to invite your town-bred friends to stay and improve the local society."

Mr. Smithson smiled ruefully. "I suppose it is. Do you come with us to Torquay the day after next?"

"I should like to, now that I feel more fully recovered. I take it you will be one of the party?"

"Yes. There will be Sir Neville and Miss Trent and the Gregsons, as well. I believe Lady Pickney and the Battersleas have declined the offer – evidently too long a carriage ride for Lady Pickney and too much sea air for Lady Batterslea."

"Too much sea air?"

"It ruins the complexion most dreadfully."

"Ah yes, so it does. We shall miss them, I'm sure."

The reduced party made its way to Torquay in much the same fashion as before, with sturdy carriages and by the usual route. Once there, the party divided itself into those that desired to walk along the shore and those that sought diversion in examining the shops along the thoroughfare. Althea, despite her interest in the natural world, joined the latter group in the hopes that she might be able to slip away and continue to investigate the body on the beach. This proved more difficult than originally imagined due to the fact that Mr. Smithson seemed unwilling to leave her side.

It was finally achieved when he indicated a desire to purchase comfits at the apothecary, and Althea moved quickly down the street instead of waiting for his return. She made her way to the Blue Bottle and sought a private room and refreshment. The waitress had just taken her order when a familiar face stuck his head around the door.

"Lord George!" Althea said, suddenly aware of how much Verlyn resembled his brother. She throttled the urge to weep and smiled at him.

"I saw you come in and sought to have private speech. Have you come alone?"

"I managed to escape my party and came here in search of further information about Mr. Nettles."

Verlyn nodded and sat down in a chair opposite her. "I have been busy as well."

"But perhaps you cannot be as forthcoming as I can be with you. The man claimed his name was Cartwright, but we know that that is not his true identity. He also appears to have been to Torquay before, perhaps multiple times. There are paths that lead into Torquay that can be traveled with some speed by a man on horseback and, if I am correct, the *x* on the note actually marks the spot of the fastest route. There must have been some nefarious business Mr. Nettles sought to investigate."

Verlyn smiled. "You have been busy, indeed. I do not need to tell you, I suppose, that what I am about to say must remain with you?"

"Of course. You have my full discretion."

"I have learned that Nettles was in Torquay to investigate a potential leak of naval information to the French. The government suspects that one of our agents has turned traitor, but it has not been clear who that may be."

The waitress entered with a cold lemonade, and Verlyn ordered an ale. All conversation ceased until the door was well closed.

Verlyn said, "Nettles was likely killed by the double agent he sought to discover."

Althea nodded. "And do you think Mr. Nettles' death in Torquay was connected in some manner with Tunwell's death? For my part, I have to think it must be."

"Yes, but I don't know exactly what transpired. Tunwell was suspected of leaking information from the ministry of the Navy, so I think that he may have been the source of the information passed on to this double agent. Perhaps the agent killed him after he received his information, and then fled."

"Or perhaps Mr. Nettles killed Lord Tunwell, but was then hunted down by the double agent."

"If that is the case, then the agent has most certainly fled the area."

The waitress re-entered with Verlyn's tankard. He thanked her and paid the bill, ensuring no further interruptions. When she was gone, Althea, who had been lost in thought said, "I wonder what that piece of paper meant by *Al Andalus?*"

"Perhaps nothing. Or perhaps it was some sort of code known only to the baron. If you are correct that the lines were the back roads leading into Torquay, Tunwell may have used it for himself as a guide. Torquay would be the perfect location to meet the agent, away from the prying eyes of the other guests at Ranleigh."

"Yes, I suppose it would have." She paused and then mumbled, "But what about the boots?"

Verlyn leaned in. "Boots?"

Althea shook her head as if shaking off her reverie. There was no use telling Verlyn about the fall. He would likely press her to return to Dettamoor Park, or worse, write to his brother. Althea couldn't think of a more humiliating situation than having the Duke of Norwich return to her out of pity or concern. No, that was not to be contemplated, so she said, "It is probably nothing, but someone crept into my room one night in order to steal a pair of boots, and I have been struggling to understand why."

"A servant?"

"I do not know, but perhaps you are correct. Servants likely feel the need of sturdy boots more than we do. Forget I mentioned it."

They conversed for several minutes more, exchanging ideas about the double agent, and then devolving into more general conversation about Torquay. Althea longed to ask about the duke, but Verlyn seemed wholly occupied with the problems at hand and didn't mention him. Althea had to assume from his easy manners that Verlyn understood the engagement to still be in place, which was some consolation, but more likely indicated that the duke hadn't seen fit to confide his amorous struggles to a younger brother.

They finished their drinks and Verlyn said, "I am staying at the inn called the Ox and Four here in Torquay under the name of Wainwright. You can send word to me there if you see or hear anything that may be of use to my investigation." Verlyn instructed her to leave first, as he would follow once he had had a chance to ask Big Meg a question. Figuring that this question was likely to be related to their previous conversation, Althea obeyed his directions.

Once outside again, she was hailed by Mr. Smithson, "Lady Trent, I am so glad to have found you!"

"Forgive me, Mr. Smithson, but I was parched with thirst and merely sought to quench it. Where are the other members of the party?"

"They are just now taking a light refreshment at the inn on First Street. I had come to look for you." He held out his arm.

Althea unfurled her parasol and laid her hand lightly upon his elbow. "Then I have been precipitate. Let us lose no more time."

After some trifling purchases in the shops and a further walk along the beach path, the party returned to Ranleigh in high spirits.

CHAPTER TWENTY-TWO

For some time, Sir Neville had promised the neighborhood a large fete to be held in and around the rose garden of Ranleigh, and the day scheduled for that merriment was a week following the trip to Torquay. As he had been successful in his pursuit of Jane, it was now also to form the local coming out of Jane as the future Lady Tabard. Jane was surprisingly anxious about the event, and so Althea spent her week pleasurably engaged in helping Jane to attend to all the petty details that were required in order to make such an event a resounding success.

This whirlwind of activity soothed Althea's heartache like nothing else because it prevented her from any quiet contemplation. In fact, the only activity to which she could devote herself, outside of attending to Jane, was the perusal of a long and detailed letter from Mr. Read. The Magistrate of Bow Street was delighted with her further experiments, not only as an exercise in scientific categorization, but also in its potential uses for crime detection. He urged her most pointedly to prepare the data for submission to the *Philosophical Transactions* of the Royal Society and also to prepare further education and training materials for his Principal Officers. He informed her that he knew of no aquatic equivalent for the Trent Method, asking her most pointedly to develop one, if she could.

Thus distracted by Jane and encouraged by Mr. Read, Althea awoke on the day of the garden party prepared to enjoy herself to the fullest extent possible. She dressed in a simple but elegant garment that Miss Dorkins praised as *the finest muslin this side of London,* figured with embroidered yellow roses and Brussels lace. Her hair was done simply – Miss Dorkins having been schooled in the London fashions that Althea had brought home to Dettamoor Park – and topped with a straw bonnet that was the envy of the other female guests.

Jane had also taken great pains to look her best, choosing a rose-colored gown that gave her cheeks the pink glow of youth, and when they met together in Althea's room, they praised one another with extravagant abandon.

"I do hope I shall make a good impression," Jane added, "for I know in what esteem Sir Neville is held by his neighbors."

Althea kissed her cheek. "You will be the belle of the ball, my dear Jane. And I am sure that any choice of Sir Neville's will be well received. He seems to have quite a reputation for fairness and generosity in these parts."

Jane smiled. "Well, you know I have always spoken my mind with some frankness, and I don't know that I was always aware of his good qualities, but, coming to Ranleigh, I realize that Sir Neville has changed. There is a new dignity that suits him. Do you not perceive it?"

Althea squeezed her hand, feeling that this comment was but one step on the path towards falling in love. "Oh yes, I do. But I feel the country is not to be identified as the cause. I think it is your beneficial influence. You are such a rational creature that I'm sure Sir Neville must hew to your example."

"Now you are teasing me," Jane replied, but blushed just the same.

The observation that Jane's heart was following the lead of her head in selecting Sir Neville as the partner of her future life was borne out as the garden party unfolded during the whole of the afternoon. Althea remained by Jane's side as her adjunct – managing the introductions to any number of persons, attending to guests, and generally making herself agreeable to all. The compliments to the happy couple flowed freely, and more than one person told Althea in a low voice that it was delightful that Sir Neville had finally thought to marry someone, after declining the charms of the local beauties for years.

So it was that, attached to Jane and Sir Neville, Althea did not have much interaction with her own party. In fact, as the afternoon wore on, she realized that she hadn't seen the new baron or Lady Batterslea at all. Perhaps they were stealing some moments alone. That was dangerous business. Lord Batterslea was not apparently the most astute of husbands, but even a simpleton must come to understand if they went about their business in an obvious fashion.

Althea's speculation was cut short when Lord Tunwell appeared suddenly at her elbow, pulling her aside. "And how have you been getting on with the neighborhood society?"

She scanned his appearance. There was nothing out of place or irregular in his dress or manner. In fact, he was remarkably and amazingly handsome. Althea noted with some amusement that many feminine eyes were turned in her direction, but, unfortunately for them, she and Cruikshank were just out of earshot, and so they couldn't eavesdrop.

"Quite well," Althea replied. "Sir Neville has the blessing of living in a neighborhood of extremely agreeable people."

"Yes, entirely agreeable when entertained in grand style by Sir Neville. I am sure in other circumstances, they will display all of the natural rivalries and bitterness of a country neighborhood."

"I think you wrong them, but I suppose that you have not had much experience living outside of London. You may think very differently once you have spent an extended period of time at Tunwell Court."

He shuddered. "Do not condemn me to such a terrible fate. I have half a mind to mortgage the lot and live in greater style abroad."

"Even with the war at fever pitch? I own that I give thanks to have been born an Englishwoman and so escape the suffering of my fellow creatures on the continent."

"It has been my experience that money makes all things possible."

Althea eyed him critically. "I suppose it must be so, if you think it."

He tossed his head back and laughed. "You have such a fine way of taking me to task. I swear, I have not a met a woman who can do it so delightfully." Then, as if suddenly impelled to speak, he added, "Come, Lady Trent, and be my wife – you and I were meant for one another. Norwich would bore you to death in a fortnight and you know it."

"You cannot be serious," she replied, with some asperity.

He met her eyes and held them with his own. "Of course I am serious. Surely, you do not think that a man of my reputation utters such declarations often?"

"If I listened to gossip, I would respond that you certainly are not above asking a woman to marry you when it suits your purpose. Whether you mean it after you have achieved your aim is another story."

"But see, that is the difference. You are not to be seduced by a lot of flowery language, so we meet as equals."

"I am afraid I still must decline. Besides, you do not know what a shrew I might become in time. I am not one of those women who could easily overlook the casual dalliances you so delight in. You would grow to hate me, and I you."

"A man does not need casual dalliance when he has a woman like you."

"Thank you for the compliment, such as it is, but I doubt that the habits of a lifetime may be cast off so easily. No, Lord Tunwell, do not tease me further."

He was about to reply, but they were interrupted by Mr. Smithson, who approached them to ask when the fete was scheduled to end. He sighed languorously. "For I have been ogled by every country bumpkin and flouncy dairy maid in all of Devonshire. It does my tailor credit, I am sure, but fatigues me to no end."

"Perhaps you had better have dressed with less style and more discretion," Cruikshank said, with a thinly-veiled sneer. "That waistcoat with the columns and lions for instance – what is it meant to be?"

"It is Hercules, is it not? The pillars of Hercules," Althea said.

Mr. Smithson smiled at her. "Clearly Lady Trent understands the classical allusion."

"Yes, but none of these good people is like to, and neither are most of the fellows in London. You cannot dress in this fashion and then complain when you are stared at. It is not for nothing that you are called *L'Incroyable*," Cruikshank said.

Mr. Smithson pulled himself up to his full height. "I am called such a name because I am indeed incredible – a paragon of taste and refinement. But then you have been on the fringes of polite society, so one cannot wonder that you fail to understand my exalted position in it."

Althea, sensing trouble, stepped between them and with a steady voice said, "Gentlemen. The day has been long and you are likely suffering from the noise and the heat. I suggest that you both return to the house and seek repose."

Each seemed to think better of continuing the argument in public, and Mr. Smithson turned on his heel and walked in the direction of the house.

"Insufferable idiot," Cruikshank said, when he was out of earshot.

"Is he really called *L'Incroyable?*" Althea said.

"Oh yes. It is a wonder he can find a tailor in all of England willing to risk his reputation and turn Smithson out in such a style."

"As you have so rightly put it – money makes all things possible – even Hercules waistcoats."

He nodded. "Not everything. Or at least, so it seemed to me before we were so rudely interrupted. Take all the time you need to consider my offer, Lady Trent. It will still be there when you tire of Norwich's games."

Althea felt that the conversation had gone far enough and was just about to give him another set down when all of the threads that had been floating in the air suddenly knit themselves together. The Pillars of Hercules! It could not be. And yet, what better disguise would there be for a brilliant man? Verlyn would be able to confirm her suspicions with his superiors. She had to get word to him immediately.

"Lady Trent, what has happened? You look unwell," Cruikshank said.

She clutched her head. "I am sorry, but I think the heat has gotten to me. I must return to the house."

He took her arm. "Here, let me escort you."

She allowed him to lead her in, but sent him away as soon as Miss Dorkins appeared to take her upstairs. Once in her room, her air of languor ceased. "No, no, there is no need to assist me to lie down. There is work to be done." She sat down and pulled a sheet of paper from her writing desk. "I need you to have one of the stable boys take this note to Mr. Wainwright at the Ox and Four in Torquay. It is most urgent."

"Who is Mr. Wainwright?" Miss Dorkins said.

"He is just a man I met in Torquay."

"I do not understand."

"Nor do I, at least not everything." She folded the note and then sealed it with red wax. "I must insist that you tell nothing of this to anyone, even Miss Jane. It is a matter of life and death."

"Life and death? Oh my! What trouble have you gotten yourself into now, Lady Trent?"

Althea smiled and handed it to her. "I know that I am a great trial. Now run along quickly. Take some coins from my reticule to pay for the servant's kindness. I will pretend to rest until you come back and tell me that the errand is accomplished. And thank you."

Miss Dorkins tucked the note in her apron and hurried out of the door. Althea sat down to wait in nervous agitation. After half an hour, Miss Dorkins rushed into the room, hot and flustered. "It is done, Lady Trent. Peter took off with it to Torquay. He had the horse saddled so quickly, I could not believe it. He is a good steady lad and so obliging. You can be sure he will do just as you ask. And I told him to send you word when he had returned."

"Thank you again, dear Miss Dorkins. Now, do not let me keep you from the fete. I will stay quietly here while you are off to enjoy your day once more."

Miss Dorkins demurred, but Althea insisted, and was finally able to push her out the door. Althea sighed and sank gratefully into a chair. So much to be done and so little time.

CHAPTER TWENTY-THREE

That night, after Peter had returned from completing his errand, Althea partook of a light supper in her room. It was better to feign illness for a time in order to make it plausible. She retired early as well, and found to her surprise that she was indeed very tired. Unfortunately, as soon as her head hit the pillow, her mind switched on, relentlessly turning over the pieces of the puzzle, but to no logical effect. She forced her thoughts back to Dettamoor Park, but that was not safe, either.

Soon they would be off to Dettamoor Park to prepare for Jane's wedding. Then Jane was to go to the Lake District for her bridal tour and then back here to her new home at Ranleigh. Althea would be left alone at Dettamoor Park to mourn the loss of a beloved sister. She felt the tears form but brushed them away before they could run down her cheek. She had never suffered long from low spirits in the past, even when her beloved father had left her too soon, or when Arthur had breathed his last. Neither of them would have wanted her to pine, and so she did her best to fill her days with reading and experiments, sure that the dull ache in her chest would ease over time.

And so it had. And so it would have to again. Jane would never come back and neither would Norwich. Althea had to be honest with herself, at least. There was no other rational explanation for his silence except that he meant, through absence, to wean her from their engagement. Althea was just going to have to focus on her scientific interests once more until time healed her heart and calmed her mind.

She was just drifting off to sleep, lulled by the thought of aquatic experiments of every type, when she heard a faint noise, like soft slippers on the drugget in the hall. Her body tensed and her eyes popped open. The room was so dark that she could not see beyond the narrow opening in the bed curtains. Was her nocturnal visitor come again? What more could he or she wish to steal? Perhaps the thief had a more nefarious purpose in mind.

It could even be Cruikshank, she reasoned, come to seduce her with kisses instead of with words. She would scream at the top of her lungs if he so much as tried to embrace her. She smiled at the vision of Cruikshank, who she was sure had never met much resistance, suddenly attacked by a hysterical female.

She heard the door creak open and saw the flicker of a candle. She half closed her eyes, imitating sleep until she knew what her visitor was about. She heard the sound of something being placed on a table in the corner. From the way the light shifted, it must be the candle. The shuffling feet approached the bed, and Althea closed her eyes completely. She felt the sudden draft of air as the bed curtains opened. And then something soft around her face, pressed down so as to cut off her breath.

Althea sat up, startling the intruder, who staggered back and dropped what appeared to be a bolster. It was a woman, by the looks of it. Althea scrambled out of bed, pressing her advantage. The woman turned to flee, but Althea lunged at her, grabbing the hem of her nightdress, and pulled her down to the floor. Althea straddled her shoulders and used the force of Althea's own weight to pinion her.

"Let me go!" the woman wheezed.

"I had not thought you a murderess, Lady Batterslea. Pray tell, what is the cause of this midnight intrusion?" Althea replied.

Jane threw open the door from her room, with Miss Dorkins right behind her. She held her candle high. "Althea! What are you doing to poor Lady Batterslea?"

"Poor Lady Batterslea! See that bolster over there? She tried to smother me."

Jane set her candle on the table. "I doubt she will try to do so again after your manhandling. Come, get off of her. Here, Miss Dorkins, help me."

Jane and Miss Dorkins helped Althea up and then extended a hand to the now petulant Lady Batterslea. "It was all your fault, you know!" she said. "If you hadn't made eyes at him like a common hussy!"

"What are you talking about?" Jane said sharply.

Lady Batterslea, finally cowed by the sharpness and authority of Jane's tone, crossed her arms in front of her and started to cry.

"I think what she means is that I am her competition for Lord Tunwell's affections. That, of course, is entirely ridiculous, but I doubt Lady Batterslea has ever had any competition where the other sex is concerned. Am I right?"

Lady Batterslea turned her head away and refused to answer, sniffing loudly in the manner of an aggrieved child.

"Well, I hardly see that the new baron is worth smothering Althea over. What can you have been thinking?" Jane said.

"Perhaps that, as the fall hadn't finished me off, a pillow would do the trick. Were you the kind person who gave me a shove off the precipice?" Althea said.

Lady Batterslea swung around and cried hotly, "I did not! Ask anyone, I was on the other side of the ruin listening to a very boring story from that awful Lady Pickney! I didn't know anything about the fall until I heard all of the commotion about it. I swear!"

"Please don't," Jane replied dryly. "Now, I suggest you do the sensible thing and return to your room, while Lady Trent and I figure out what is best to be done."

Lady Batterslea stopped her sniffles and said in a wheedling voice, "But you won't tell Lord Batterslea about me and Lord Tunwell, will you?"

Althea was about to reply, but Jane cut her off. "We haven't decided yet. Go back to bed before you wake the house."

Lady Batterslea hesitated and sought perhaps to persuade them further, but Jane took Lady Batterslea's arm and said firmly, "Come, I will help you to your room."

When Jane returned, she dismissed Miss Dorkins and indicated that Althea should sit.

"I find your masterful handling of midnight murderesses quite delightful, you know," Althea said.

Jane sat down. "Althea. Althea. How is it possible that you can have gotten yourself in such a state?"

"I certainly have done nothing to encourage either Cruikshank's attentions or Lady Batterslea's jealousy."

"No, I am aware of that. Yet somehow trouble finds you more than it does others."

"Do you think Lady Batterslea was telling the truth when she said she didn't push me?" Althea said.

"While a woman who would smother another over a man would likely have no problem in pushing someone down a hill, I think I remember her standing beside us while Lady Pickney regaled us with one of her society stories. Then again, she could have slipped away. I was paying attention to Lady Pickney, so I cannot be sure."

"Should we make Lord Batterslea aware of his wife's activities?" Althea said.

"I don't know that we can, with any degree of success. He is besotted, poor man, and in any case, she would deny the whole to him."

"Yes, but I don't think we should let her know that. If she fears discovery, she may refrain from murdering me."

Jane smiled. "Unless she murders us both."

"But then Miss Dorkins must explain the whole to the magistrate," Althea pointed out.

"Poor Miss Dorkins. She doesn't deserve such trials."

"I wonder if Lady Batterslea was connected to the death of the previous Lord Tunwell?"

"How could she be connected?" Jane said.

"Perhaps this affair with the new lord is of long standing and she sought to promote her lover's interests? If she were to leave Batterslea and run to Cruikshank, it would be better that he had a title and money to support her. Perhaps the murder was her way of proving her love to him."

"But, assuming that the previous baron was murdered, which I still cannot believe, how could Lady Batterslea push him into the water to drown him? He was large enough to fend for himself."

"What if he slipped and she took advantage of the situation in order to hold him under?" Althea said.

"But they arrived after the baron was found dead."

"Yes, so we were told."

"You know that a woman is circumscribed in her movements. She could hardly come ahead of her husband without his knowledge and commit murder. He would certainly know of it."

Althea thought for a moment. "Then maybe Batterslea does know of it. What if she told him that she was coming to break off her relationship with Mr. Cruikshank?"

"But he was not invited to Ranleigh."

"True, but perhaps she convinced him that he would be if his uncle was clearly invited."

"An uncle he was not on speaking terms with?" Jane said.

Althea laughed. "Jane, you have no mercy, do you?"

"Not when you are spouting nonsensical ideas. Why does the baron's death have to be connected to everything that has happened to you? In my mind, it is not. Lord Tunwell died as a result of an accident. We found the body in Torquay by chance. A servant misplaced her mistress's boots and sought to get them back without anyone knowing of her carelessness. You leaned too far over the hill and fell. Lady Batterslea attacked you in a separate fit of jealousy. The only common thread is your penchant for trouble."

"You make it seem so commonplace! And yet I am not convinced. Let me work it out on my own."

Jane stood up. "As you wish. I hate to ask it, but do you think you could hold your tongue about Lady Batterslea until I have a moment to speak with Sir Neville? I wish to consult with him before we take any action against guests in his house."

"I agree. Sir Neville must be consulted. In any case, I shall take care to be gone most of the day tomorrow so that I shall not tempt Lady Batterslea to make another attempt."

"Where will you go?"

"I have some errands in the village."

Jane sought for further information, but Althea preferred to keep her own counsel. The less Jane knew of Althea's thoughts on the subject of threads, the better. It was time for investigation into at least one of her numerous theories.

CHAPTER TWENTY-FOUR

The next morning, Althea rose early, breakfasted, and then called for her carriage. She was just about to enter the carriage when a footman handed her a missive folded in two and sealed with black wax. She broke the seal and read Lord George's hurried scrawl.

"Is the messenger who brought this still around?" she asked the footman.

When the footman answered in the affirmative, she asked for the messenger to be brought to her. He turned out to be a young lad not more than twelve. "Milady has a message for the gentleman what sent me?"

"Yes. Tell him to meet me at the apothecary at midday. Thank you very much." She removed a coin from her reticule and gave it to him.

He grinned at her. "Yes, milady. I'll tell him straight away."

Althea arrived at the village and set about her inquiries. She had no luck at the small lending library, but the young woman at the marzipan shop had some useful, although not precise, recollections. Althea then made several small purchases at the hat shop, but managed to avoid the ugly bonnet, in order so as not to appear conspicuous. At the appointed hour, she entered the apothecary shop. Inside the shop stood an elderly woman in a tense discussion with the apothecary about the best remedy for a persistent cough and Verlyn, pretending to examine a clear glass jar full of leeches.

Althea came over to him and said in a low voice. "I know *Al Andalus* is the code name of a spy and I know who he is. The question is, why did Lord Tunwell have his name on a piece of paper?"

"I think I may have the answer to that question," he replied.

There was a sudden commotion at the door. Althea turned. "Why, Mr. Smithson, I had not expected to see you in the village. Did you come to do some shopping?"

Smithson smiled broadly and approached them. He had on a greatcoat with capes over his usual splendid attire, his right hand deep in the coat pocket. "Ah, Lord George Verlyn and dear Lady Trent, how delightful!"

As he came near, Althea could see that his coat pocket was pushed outward in a strange manner. Smithson saw the direction of her gaze and said in a low voice, barely audible above the sound of the elderly lady. "Yes, that is a pistol in my pocket. If you and Lord George would be so kind as to accompany me out the door, I would be much obliged. I do not wish to kill that poor unfortunate woman with her terrible cough, although perhaps I should, if only to put her out of her misery."

Althea looked at Verlyn, who nodded and took her arm. "Come, Lady Trent, let us walk with Mr. Smithson for a little while," he said loudly.

Smithson motioned them ahead of him and out the door. It clanged behind them. "Where to, Smithson?" asked Verlyn, without so much as a quiver in his voice. He squeezed Althea's arm in reassurance and she began to wonder just how often Verlyn found himself is such situations.

"I think we should continue on away from Ranleigh. I will tell you when to stop," Smithson said.

Verlyn started walking slowly and then he began to make commonplace conversation about the village and the shops and the fine weather. It was as if he didn't have a care in the world. Althea marveled at his composure and sought to emulate his serene countenance. All the while, her brain ran feverishly from one possibility to the next. Smithson had to be the murderer, despite all of her conjecture to the contrary. How had she been so wrong? It was too fantastic, and yet, she had to admit it had a certain neatness of resolution. All of the possibilities tied together in one tidy package. Magistrate Read would be enthralled – if she lived long enough to tell him about it.

Finally, they reached the outskirts of the village, beyond the blacksmith's shop and some isolated houses. They entered a lane that ran into a large copse of trees, and when they attained the end of it, Mr. Smithson said, "I think we may safely speak here. Turn around."

He removed the gun from his pocket and pointed it at Lord George. It was a small pistol, but likely deadly at close range. Just the sort of pistol to have put a bullet in a man's head and left him to the mercy of the waves.

"Now, Verlyn, why don't you explain to me why you have been hiding out in Torquay and why you have taken such pains to investigate the death of that man on the beach? I have had such a time following you around. It is most disconcerting."

"You are *Al Andalus*," Althea interjected.

Mr. Smithson hesitated, seemingly uncertain as to how to respond. "Yes, Lady Trent, I am, but how or why you came to know this, I have yet to discover. Please enlighten me so that I will not make the same mistake again."

"It was your waistcoat. The Pillars of Hercules represent Gibraltar and that is on the tip of Spain. And Spain is *Al Andalus*. I realized that it could be the name of a person when I found out my horse was named Andalusia. And then I heard that you were called *L'Incroyable* and the ideas fitted themselves together."

"But how did you even know about *Al Andalus*?" Smithson said. "Really, your statement amazes me."

"I believe I can enlighten you there, Smithson." Verlyn reached up and pulled out a piece of paper from a pocket cleverly concealed inside his waistcoat. He handed it to Smithson, who took it with his other hand, all the while keeping the pistol pointing steadily in his direction.

Smithson looked at the paper and then looked back at Verlyn, surprise writ large across his face. "For the love of God, why didn't you tell me?" He brought the pistol down and tucked it back into his pocket. "And I was prepared to shoot dear Lady Trent, too!"

"You didn't give us much choice, did you?" Verlyn replied.

Smithson handed the paper back to him. "No, but you could have said something before now. And how is Lady Trent involved in all this, unless the government has now entrusted such work to females?"

"Lady Trent has been quite helpful to our government," Verlyn replied gallantly. "You may speak freely in front of her. She found a note on the body of Lord Tunwell that led us to believe that he had an interest in Torquay and some-one or something named *Al Andalus*."

"Ah, so that was it! Forgive me, Lady Trent, for frightening you just now, but I have been at a loss to understand your movements as well. I suspected that you were hunting something, but what it was, I could not tell. And when I intercepted your notes and discovered you were meeting Verlyn here, I had to take you with me, so to speak."

"My principal purpose was to determine who killed Lord Tunwell. I thought it perhaps had to do with the note I found, and then later, with the man on the beach. I see that I was correct in this. If I may ask, Mr. Smithson, just how did you manage to wrestle Lord Tunwell into the water? And once you had done so, were you intending that I should find the body? I seem to remember that you tried to dissuade me from going near the pond and investigating the odd shape in the reeds." Althea said.

"No, I had no notion either way. You see, I had meant to kill Lord Tunwell myself, but someone or something got there ahead of me."

"So, Lord Tunwell was leaking secrets to a French agent?" Verlyn said.

"Yes, secrets that included my name and other details of our naval strategy. I was sent to discover the truth and then to kill him, if I found it necessary. Unfortunately, when I went to look for him, I found him dead. There was nothing to be done."

"Except to murder his accomplice in Torquay," Verlyn said.

Althea turned to him. "Mr. Nettles!"

"Yes," Verlyn smiled ruefully. "I had to seek guidance from London in order to understand the whole. It appears that Smithson here is one of a small cadre of agents whose existence is kept secret from the rest of us, unless the occasion calls for it."

"And you from me, Verlyn. While I understand the secrecy, I have wasted a great deal of valuable time following you and Lady Trent around. It would have been so much easier if we could have worked together."

"So, how did you discover that the agent in Torquay had betrayed his country?" Althea asked.

Smithson sighed. "It was a sad bit of theater. Mr. Nettles always appeared in Torquay when the baron came to stay at Ranleigh. We knew we had a mole in the service, and that someone was leaking documents from highly confidential sources. It was merely a matter of putting two and two together."

Althea nodded. "And you conveniently received an invitation to Ranleigh this summer."

Smithson smiled. "I am a very affable person, Lady Trent. Sir Neville merely recognized my admirable qualities as a friend and confidant."

"I see," Althea replied.

"In any case, I had thought to clear off once I had taken care of Nettles, but then I had the pair of you acting peculiar, and so I determined to learn the whole."

Althea shuddered. "I am glad you asked questions first before you took care of us. We might have joined Mr. Nettles in his fate."

"I make it a rule to be particularly careful in my position. Death is so very messy, and I abhor a mess," Mr. Smithson said.

"It wasn't you who pushed me down the hill?"

"Someone pushed you down a hill?" Verlyn said.

"And here I thought you were just particularly clumsy," Smithson said.

"I am not clumsy, and yes, I felt a distinct push before I went over the edge."

"No, dear Lady Trent, I was not involved in anything so vulgar. I am a trained assassin. If I had meant to kill you, I would have done it properly. Besides, I was enthralled by one of Lady Pickney's delightful stories at the time."

"But, apart from Smithson here, why would anyone want to hurt you, Lady Trent?" Verlyn asked.

Althea decided not to bring up Lady Batterslea or her midnight visitor and so she said airily, "I can see no reason why anyone would."

"The person who murdered Lord Tunwell might take the same exception I took to your little investigations," Smithson said.

"I think it is time that I returned to Ranleigh," Verlyn said.

"If this is an attempt to keep watch over me, then I will respectfully decline. I am on my guard now and so can handle any purported attempt to harm me," Althea said.

Verlyn seemed doubtful, but Smithson said, "There is no need for that black look, Verlyn. Now that I know what Lady Trent is about, I can keep my eyes and ears alert to any plot. Besides, it will give me some occupation until I am to visit friends in the North, now that my duties on behalf of his majesty's government have ceased for the moment."

Verlyn replied, "I concede then, and would be most grateful, as I have some business to conclude. When do you plan to journey north?"

"The date is fixed a fortnight hence," Smithson said.

"And when do you return to Dettamoor Park, Lady Trent?" Verlyn asked.

Althea, wrapped up in her own thoughts, answered absently, "Three full weeks."

"Then, I shall schedule my return to Ranleigh accordingly," Verlyn said. "Now that that issue is settled, perhaps we should make our way back?"

The three of them walked together to the edge of the village and Verlyn took his leave.

Althea offered Mr. Smithson a ride back in her carriage, but he declined. "I certainly didn't walk to the village! My heavens, what must you think of me? My horse is with the ostler at the inn."

Althea smiled, suddenly sure of her course. "Sorry if I have offended you. Perhaps you would be so good as to give me your arm back to my carriage? I have an idle question or two about your birthplace. I have traveled so little that each new place is a delight to discuss."

CHAPTER TWENTY-FIVE

When the party returned, the rest of the company had just been invited to some alfresco refreshments in the rose garden. Althea hurried up to change her dress and then joined the group. Mr. Smithson came down several minutes later, resplendent in a dark blue jacket and striped silk waistcoat and skin tight yellow pantaloons. The polish on his boots was like a looking glass. Knowing what she now knew about his clandestine activities, Althea had trouble reconciling the ruthless assassin with the dandy now before her.

Upon seeing Mr. Smithson, Lady Pickney exclaimed, "My dear sir, I don't know how you manage to look so crisp and cool as you always do!" She fanned her pink cheeks. "Why, even out here in the shade, it is very warm."

"It is a gift, Lady Pickney, I assure you," he replied with a bland smile.

Lady Pickney chuckled. "So, I believe it must be. That reminds me of a story my father used to tell about Sir Horace Trowley." She proceeded to tell a rather long but highly amusing anecdote involving an elderly dandy, a mule and a milkmaid, which had the desired effect of keeping the party entertained until the refreshments were thoroughly consumed and some of the guests mentioned retiring for a little repose before the exertions of supper.

Althea was in no mood to rest and so informed the party that she was going to take a walk around the pond, assuming that none of the other guests would find that sufficiently exciting to follow her, thus leaving her alone to pursue her thoughts, devise a strategy for catching a murderer, and make new scientific observations.

In any case, she was thwarted in her attempts at solitude because Cruikshank expressed a desire to accompany her. This created a domino effect. Lady Batterslea, stung by jealousy, declared her intention to come. This forced Mr. Smithson, in light of his promise to Verlyn, to agree to make one of the party. Then Mrs. Gregson, obviously seeing that half the group was engaged in activity and desiring not to be left behind, expressed her wish to join the group, as well.

Thus arranged, the party entered the house and changed into clothes suitable for a walk on a warm summer afternoon. They met down in the hall, and set out at a sedate pace. Cruikshank maneuvered until Althea found herself sandwiched between him and Mr. Smithson, the other two ladies following slightly behind. Then Lady Batterslea came up beside them and claimed Cruikshank's attention, forcing him to slow his pace and fall behind. Mrs. Gregson moved forward and took her place to Althea's right.

The group passed into a copse of trees, refreshed by the cool of the shade. Mrs. Gregson chattered on about inconsequential subjects, blithely unaware of where she walked until she tripped on a tree root and Althea grabbed her arm. It was in that moment that Althea caught a flash of brown leather and her suspicions were confirmed. It all fell together. Althea took a deep breath to steady herself.

"Oh my lord, I am the clumsiest creature," Mrs. Gregson said, standing up straight and shaking out her skirt. "Thank you, Lady Trent, for catching me."

Althea schooled her features into a bland smile. "It was nothing, I assure you."

The others joined them, and they passed out of the copse into the open, under the warmth of a blazing sun. The pond shimmered in front of them, not two hundred feet away.

Then there was a sudden commotion. Althea turned around and saw Lady Batterslea fall backwards into Cruikshank's arms with the air of someone who desires to cause a sensation. He caught her and, startled, lay her gently onto the ground. Mr. Smithson, clearly suspecting some trick, called her name loudly, and when that didn't seem to rouse her, removed a scented handkerchief and waved it in the air above her. Althea and Mrs. Gregson hurried over just in time to see Lady Batterslea flutter her eyelids open.

"Oh, dear. What can have happened?" she said in a husky whisper.

Cruikshank, who had been the obvious recipient of the communication, replied, "You appear to have fainted, Lady

Batterslea. Here, Mr. Smithson, please help me. We must assist Lady Batterslea to arise."

Althea, who suspected that Lady Batterslea had actually desired to be carried in Cruikshank's arms as she had once been carried by Norwich, crouched down and took Lady Batterslea's wrist in her fingers. Just as suspected, her pulse was strong and steady. "I think you will rapidly recover if you can travel to a location away from the sun and heat."

"Yes," Lady Batterslea said with a tremulous voice. "I think that I should return. Perhaps Lord Tunwell, you would be so kind as to help me to walk back to Ranleigh?"

"Perhaps, if Mr. Smithson would assist me," Lord Tunwell said, "For I think Lady Batterslea may need an arm on her other side."

Smithson sighed and gave Althea a fleeting look. Althea nodded slightly, encouraging him to leave her and assist Lady Batterslea.

The men helped her to rise and then stationed themselves on either arm. Lady Batterslea was not very well pleased, but put on a good face.

Mrs. Gregson turned to Althea. "I think we should go with them."

"Please, by all means," Althea replied with a smile, "but I think I will carry on with my walk to the pond. My time at Ranleigh is growing short, and I do not wish to give up such a lovely afternoon. I am sure Lady Batterslea cannot come to harm with two such companions."

Mrs. Gregson gave Althea a hard look, as if taking her measure, and then said, "As you wish, Lady Trent."

Althea watched her walk away and then turned towards the pond. She desperately needed time to think and to plan.

It was all clear to her now, except for the manner and the method to bring about justice. The local magistrate could be called, but would be unlikely to listen to an eccentric widow. She would have to explain the matter to Mr. Read first so that he could vouch for the truth of her accusations.

Althea stood at the edge of the water, watching the sun glint off of its surface, wholly engrossed in her own meditations. She heard the faint sound of the swish of fabric between legs. So, the reckoning would come before she could explain it all to Mr. Read. Very well! She spun on her heel and faced Mrs. Gregson. That lady took a step backwards in surprise.

"Lady Trent, I thought better of going back."

"I think you will find Mr. Smithson enough to keep Lord Tunwell out of Lady Batterslea's clutches for today. Although the damage has already been done."

Mrs. Gregson's sharp eyes fixed on her face and then flitted away again. "I'm not sure I take your meaning, Lady Trent."

"Merely, that he has already engaged in a dalliance with her. But do not be too perturbed. I think he means to be done with her when the summer ends. Whether she means to be done with him is another matter, of course."

Mrs. Gregson gave a high false laugh. "You do say the drollest things, Lady Trent. I really have no interest in Lord Tunwell."

Althea smiled. "Let us not mince words. I think you have a great deal of interest in Lord Tunwell and his uncle before him. In fact, I think you took such an interest that you persuaded the late baron to maintain him as his heir despite the many occasions he sought to disinherit poor Mr.

Cruikshank. Now why you would go to all that trouble, I do not understand. Unless perhaps you were very attached to his late mother?"

"I was very fond of Dorothea Cruikshank, yes, and Livia, the late Lady Tunwell, also. We grew up together, you see, so there is no great mystery in that."

"On the contrary, there is a great deal of mystery as to why your fondness for the mother and the aunt of Mr. Cruikshank should lead you to kill the baron on his behalf? It seems a fearful step to take merely for the sake of fondness."

"Kill Lord Tunwell on Mr. Cruikshank's behalf? I think that the sun has affected you as well, Lady Trent."

"You can mock me all you like, but the evidence does not lie. You really shouldn't have come back for those boots. They tell the whole sordid tale."

"What boots?"

"The boots you wore when you pushed the baron into the pond and drowned him. The ones that were then quickly cleaned by the house staff without a thought, but which were mistakenly returned to me instead of you. The boots that despite cleaning retained the dirt and plant matter from the pond between the sole and the heel. The ones you are now wearing upon your feet."

Mrs. Gregson looked down and stuck out a foot. "These old things? Why, I have had them forever. I don't know what you are talking about."

"Then let me enlighten you. They are new boots, for one thing – the soles are hardly worn. I suspect you bought them for your visit to Ranleigh. And I suspect that you found it very bothersome when they went missing. I remember you told me that you enjoyed a long walk. But somehow I never saw you walk the grounds. I think that is because you didn't have your boots. I have to assume that your husband noticed that they were missing and, being very tight fisted, gave you no end of trouble about them. That is why you had to come into my room at night and steal them back."

Mrs. Gregson opened her mouth in a smile that showed most of her teeth. "Again, I am not sure what you can possibly mean, Lady Trent."

"Do you know that when you dig a pond you bring up layers of earth? Those layers may be quite different than the topsoil of the lawn, for example, or the dust of the gravel paths. So different, in fact, that a careful study of the dirt trapped in the heel of your boot indicated that you could only have acquired that dirt from wading into the pond."

"Dirt? You talk of dirt? That is no evidence of anything!"

"Perhaps not." Althea walked to the edge of the pond and snapped off the end of a reed. She handed it to Mrs. Gregson. "However, the piece of banded horsetail trapped with the dirt proves the case. There is no way that a reed of this type came to be lodged between the heel and the sole of your boot, unless you had waded into the pond."

Mrs. Gregson threw the reed on the ground. "And even if all you say is true, who would believe you?"

"The Magistrate of Bow Street."

Mrs. Gregson finally showed a hint of fear. "And how does the Magistrate of Bow Street know a drab nothing of a widow?"

"He knows me quite well, actually. But do not hesitate to disbelieve me, if you like. I have given Mr. Read a full account of my investigations here. You shall not escape justice for your crime."

"My crime?" Mrs. Gregson replied angrily, finally goaded beyond her limits. "My crime? You know nothing of the sufferings she endured! My poor poor Livia! She was so young and pure, so innocent, and he gave her the most loathsome and abominable disease. The French pox, as they call it. It wracked her body. She was covered with boils!"

"But that was a long time ago. Why avenge her now?"

She took a ragged breath and continued, seeming not to have heard Althea. "Then, as if to add insult to injury, he made her take a mercury cure! Covered her with creams and filled the air with vapors. He said it would make everything right. He said she would be able to have a baby – the one thing she had always wanted – but instead, it robbed her of her faculties. She went mad! So out of her mind that she ended her days chained up in a room in the attic. Now tell me, who has committed the crime?"

"But why did the baron have her take mercury if he himself took arsenic?" Althea said.

"Because he was the most selfish being alive and desired her to try what he himself was unwilling to undergo. The doctors told him that mercury would cure him more rapidly. He feared for his own safety, but thought nothing of risking hers." She looked at Althea defiantly. "And that is why I had to kill him."

"But why now? Why after all these years?"

"I had my reasons."

"I see. Perhaps you needed time to plan. It must have taken some effort to ingratiate yourself enough for an invitation to Ranleigh, where you would have the freedom of movement to invite the baron to take a walk with you. After all, you were friends of old, or so he thought."

Mrs. Gregson eyed her coldly but did not disagree.

"And then you had only to learn his habits enough to know just what would tempt him. You knew from his choice of comfits that he preferred almond to other flavors. That provided the perfect opportunity to give him a taste of his own medicine. Or, more precisely, a significant overdose of the very arsenic he took as a cure, wrapped in the sticky sweetness of marzipan. The girl at the shop in Berryfield remembers you purchasing some before we arrived. Your red hair is quite distinctive."

"I should have worn a close bonnet, I suppose," Mrs. Gregson replied.

"It was very clever of you to choose arsenic, because no one could ever prove that he hadn't taken it himself. And then, while he was in a fit, you had only to push him in and hold him under. It was the perfect crime, or it would have been, had it not been for your boots getting covered in pond mud."

"You seem to have figured it all out."

"Almost everything. I am still not sure why you bothered to push me down the hill, unless I have misjudged your perspicacity. Was it merely that I had discerned too much for your comfort?"

"No, not at all. It was for the pleasure of the thing. A pleasure that would only have been equaled by your death," she said.

"And what has given you such a cause for hate?"

"Do not play the fool with me. Almost from the very moment you set eyes on him, you desired to make him your conquest. You had a duke, so I am told, and yet that was not enough. With your arts and allurements, you sought to draw him in."

"You surely cannot mean Mr. Cruikshank?" Althea said.

"Of course, I mean him. Now that he is Lord Tunwell, he was made for better things than you – an alliance with a noble house – with one of the great families of England! I could not let him fall prey to your base temptation. For you would only seek to ruin his magnificent future."

"All of this you do for your love of his mother and aunt?"

"No!" she cried out. "I did it because he is my son!"

"Your son? But how?"

"I was young, and very foolishly entered into a secret engagement. Suffice it to say that my betrothed left me with child. I confided my secret to Dorothea, who had yet to conceive a child of her own with Mr. Cruikshank. She was such a free spirit and so very kind. We contrived to travel to the continent under the pretext of visiting relatives in Burgundy. There I gave birth and she took the baby, raising him as hers. I thought that surely I would be able to have more children, but Mr. Gregson could not get me with child, the stupid ignorant man."

Mrs. Gregson began to pace, lost in her own world. "Do you know what it is like to watch your only child, the pride and joy of your life, raised by others? And then to see how the baron treated him, threatening to cast him aside, all for a little folly. Time and time again I have had to coax and persuade the baron to change his mind. Finally, I knew I had to give my son what he rightfully deserved. I planned it all so very meticulously. The marzipan and the arsenic. It was too easy. Then to see the fruits of my labor so easily overthrown. To see you worm your way into his affections. It is all too much. I tell you, I won't stand for it!"

Before Althea could leap out of the way, Mrs. Gregson took a running start and hurled herself upon her, knocking her back. She struggled to break free, but Mrs. Gregson was like a wild animal. They rolled backwards and then there was a large splash. Althea felt the cold water on her back. She struggled against her, but Mrs. Gregson was a strong woman, caught in the grip of mad rage. Althea wriggled this way and that, hopelessly tangled in the reeds. Mrs. Gregson pressed her full weight upon her and she struggled to breathe. She managed to free one arm and scratched frantically at Mrs. Gregson's face. Mrs. Gregson's startled reaction gave Althea the opportunity she needed to push off with her legs and break free of the plants encircling the pond.

Althea moved her arms and legs, happy to discover that no bones had been broken. She pushed off again, doing the movements her father had taught her long ago. Dr. Claire had attended several deaths by drowning and had not wanted any child of his to share that fate, even if swimming was not a fit thing for a girl to know. Althea silently blessed him as she moved farther out into the center of the pond, away from the clutches of Mrs. Gregson.

Mrs. Gregson lunged after her, but pulled up short, grabbing frantically at the reeds for balance. *Could it be that she did not know how to swim?* Althea watched her for a moment, treading water, waiting to see if she needed to swim farther out in order to escape, but no. Mrs. Gregson was not moving farther into the pond. She clung stubbornly to the reeds, emitting panicked little shrieks, like a forlorn child.

Althea closed her eyes and took a deep breath to steady her nerves. The water felt cold and delicious after the heat of the day.

"My God! Mrs. Gregson, Althea, what happened?"

Althea's eyes snapped open. "My lord!" Her heart seemed to stop for a second and then started up again, pounding a staccato rhythm in her chest.

Norwich was on the bank, pulling at the frantic Mrs. Gregson. "Just hold on!" he yelled, as he hauled Mrs. Gregson onto the shore. Then he tore his jacket off, pulled off his boots, and jumped into the water.

Althea opened her mouth to reply but nothing came out. She watched as his powerful frame slid through the water. He was a strong fine swimmer and reached the center of the pond with ease.

"Do not be afraid, Althea, I have you!" Then he stopped, suddenly noticing that she was not in fact drowning, but treading water. "What?"

She recovered her voice. "I can swim, but thank you just the same."

His eyes flashed in anger. "You!"

His indignation seemed somehow comical and so she let out a giggle and then, because she couldn't help it, a full-throated laugh.

He eyed her suspiciously, and, when he seemed to conclude she was not mad, laughed a little himself. "Come, we must get back to shore, Althea."

"Yes. I doubt Mrs. Gregson will have the power to kill me now."

He looked grimly at the woman still lying on the bank. "Read told me you were in some trouble. I now see that he grossly underestimated the matter."

CHAPTER TWENTY-SIX

Later that evening, after the bedraggled threesome had been allowed to clean up, and the magistrate called in to take Mrs. Gregson's confession, Althea received a note surreptitiously slipped into her reticule.

Meet me at midnight in the rose garden. I must speak with you.
N

Althea crumpled the note in her hand, a sudden fear stopping her breath. There would be no more delays. Norwich meant to end their relationship once and for all. The irony that he had now won her heart was too bitter to contemplate. Althea resolved to bury her emotions deep and carry on as if nothing had changed, as if the very sight of him sitting down to supper didn't make her feel weak with desire and longing. After a painful meal, at which she declined to answer any number of questions with the instructions the magistrate had given her not to speak of the matter with anyone until his investigation was complete, she resolutely declined tea and went to her room for an hour or two of silent contemplation.

At half past eleven, she told Miss Dorkins that she wished to take the night air because she couldn't sleep, changed into a muslin dress, and, firmly refusing Miss Dorkins' offer of company, wrapped her shawl around her shoulders. She resolutely took her candle and pulled the door closed behind her.

She found a lantern hanging beside the door at the bottom of the back stairs and lit that, leaving her extinguished candle on a small table. With the lantern held high, she threaded her way through the out buildings into the garden and then down through the gravel walks that twisted and turned until they reached the heart of the rose garden.

The air was heavy and damp, amplifying the pungent fragrance of roses that had just passed their prime blooms and settled into sickly sweetness on the way to death. *I think I shall remember this night for the rest of my life,* she thought. *The smell of the death of hope.*

She saw another light at the far end of the garden and approached it resolutely. "I thank you once again, sir, for trying to rescue me. I am sorry to have spoilt your clothes to no good purpose."

Norwich turned towards her. "It was nothing, I assure you. I wish that you would have had more care than to bait a murderess, but I suppose sensible behavior is beyond hope, at this point."

Althea looked away, stung by his cold manner. That was not the speech of a man in love. Her heart in her throat, she began quietly, sure that if she did not speak her mind at the present moment, she never would. "I am not sure in what manner I have offended you, but whatever it may have been, I am heartily sorry. Please forgive me."

"No indeed, you have done nothing to give offense." He looked at her, but avoided meeting her gaze. "I wish you joy in your marriage. I certainly could do nothing less, under the circumstances."

Her mind raced. Did he think she was in love with Cruikshank? "Wish me joy? But I fail to understand you. To whom am I betrothed, if not to you? Not that I will hold you to that promise, as it has been clear to me that you desire very much to be rid of me, but yet I do not understand."

He registered surprise and then met her eyes. "Are you not engaged to my brother?"

"Your brother? No, of course not. I am engaged to you."

"I know, but I release you."

"Fine, but I do not want to be engaged to your brother. Moreover, I do not think he wants to be engaged to me."

Norwich stared at her, his mouth open in surprise. "But you looked at him in such a way when we were in Torquay – and he kissed your hand. If that was not a sign of a betrothal, then what is?"

"I gave him a clue to the mystery of the Torquay spying ring and the body of the agent we found on the beach. He was momentarily overjoyed." Althea took a deep breath. "I know that I have not always been sure of my heart, but trust me when I say that my conversations with your brother have done nothing but reinforce the fact that I have fallen deeply and irrevocably in love with you. However, I understand if my hesitation has caused your love to sour. Indeed, it would be a wonder if it had not —"

Althea didn't finish the last word because she was seized in the grip of powerful arms. His lips found hers in an urgent plea. She responded in kind, melting into him, her desire fueled by overwhelming relief. He was as truly hers as he had ever been. She could have cried from happiness.

Sometime later, she disengaged from Norwich long enough to ask. "So you do still wish to marry me?"

"Of course I do. George is one of the few men to whom I would have relinquished the right."

"We have done nothing but speak of you —"

"I wish I would have known that. I could not contemplate your happiness together one more day, and so fled like a coward."

"You mother was not ill? When you left so suddenly, I was certain it must be because of an illness. It was only when you did not write that I began to doubt your regard for me."

"My mother is as well as ever. I meant to write, but every time I tried to set pen to paper, the words failed me. I could not ask what I did not wish to know."

"I would have corrected the mistake at once."

"Stop. I have been a fool too long. Tell me honestly, what brought you to own your regard for me?"

"If you want the truth, I missed you quite dreadfully when I thought you had thrown me off."

He smiled and kissed her gently, persuasively. "Then perhaps I should leave again."

"Please don't."

"I find you necessary for my happiness. Come, we must find a bench to sit so you can tell me everything that has happened."

"I don't know how much longer I can stay out before my reputation is quite ruined. I told Miss Dorkins that I only needed to walk a short time in order to help me sleep." She pulled her shawl close.

"Are you cold? Here, take my coat."

"No, but surely you have noticed that we have been out for more than an hour. I cannot even pretend that ours was merely a chance meeting."

He gazed at her lovingly. "I am afraid I have no notion of the hour. At first, I was too nervous to pay attention, and now a lifetime is too short for the pleasures of your company."

Althea felt her cheeks flush. She said archly, "You meant to cast me off. That would give anyone nerves."

He guided her to a bench and sat close beside her, tucking her neatly under his arm.

"I meant to release you. A very different thing. Now, before your ridiculous scruples force you to run off again, tell me again what it was that caused George to kiss your hand."

Althea gave him the complete story, not omitting the prominent role played by Mr. Smithson.

"I wish Smithson had more sense than to leave you with a murderess."

"He couldn't know. And besides, I wished to have private speech with her in order to test my theories."

"Now describe what happened with Mrs. Gregson – the complete story from start to finish. I could tell from what you had written to Magistrate Read that you left a good deal out."

Althea explained how she had come to suspect Mrs. Gregson of Lord Tunwell's death. "I originally thought that his death was connected with the spy ring, but arsenic is not the sort of poison one would use as a spy. It is too imprecise. Besides, whoever had poisoned him, knew about the arsenic he actually took, which gave it more of a domestic flavor, so to speak. Of course, I didn't suspect Mrs. Gregson was Mr. Cruikshank's mother, just her connection with his adoptive mother and aunt, for which information I am greatly indebted to Mr. Smithson. His knowledge of the northern families and their Scottish connections is incredibly detailed."

Norwich hugged her close. "Promise me you will not chase death in this fashion when we are married. I cannot contemplate the thought of losing you."

She laid her head upon his chest, feeling the beat of his heart against her cheek. "I promise I will try not to."

"In any case, I mean to marry you as soon as I have the special license, so I will keep a strict watch."

Althea sat up. "The marriage. Do you think we could be married with Jane and Sir Neville? They are to be married from Dettamoor Park in a little over a month. But perhaps your family would not like to see you married in such a place and with such company. For we have invited all of our neighbors, and Squire Pettigrew is sure to be one of the party."

He chuckled. "My family will be happy I have finally chosen a bride, and even if they are not, I shall marry when and where I choose. I would not wish Squire Pettigrew anywhere else. His pretensions to your hand must be put to rest, once and for all."

"Then it is settled," she replied. "I will write to my son and you may write to your mother, and we will be married before our six month engagement has ended. I must tell Jane."

"Not entirely settled. One thing still puzzles me. Mr. Read told me that you had some theory regarding soil. I thought he must have confused the matter, for what could soil have to do with anything?"

"I will tell you when I have more time. Now, please let us return to the house. Miss Dorkins will be beside herself with worry."

He stood up and held out his hand. "Heaven forbid we upset Miss Dorkins."

They walked hand in hand towards the house and then, as if by tacit agreement, separated, Althea entering through the back door and Norwich through the front. When Althea reached the table where her abandoned candle sat, she heard strange sounds. It could have been voices raised in anger and a wail, like a wounded animal, but from some other part of the house. Althea followed the sounds, back through the main hall and into the old wing of the house. She entered the hallway to the bedrooms and her eyes met with a scene of pandemonium.

There were two maids huddled together, sobbing into their handkerchiefs. The door to one of the bedrooms was thrown open and Cruikshank was standing in his shirtsleeves, holding a large candelabra. Lord and Lady Pickney were beside him, dressed in night clothes, to all appearances as if they had just been awakened from slumber.

"What has happened?" Althea said.

"Is that you, Althea?" Norwich called from inside the room.

"Yes." She pushed past the maids and Cruikshank through the door and found Norwich crouched down beside the lifeless form of Mrs. Gregson. Mr. Gregson was huddled on the floor, his knees tucked up to his chin like a small child, emitting a high wail of anguish.

"I heard Mr. Gregson and ran to investigate," Norwich said.

She picked up Mrs. Gregson's wrist for a pulse, but knew that there was nothing that could be done. Mrs. Gregson's lifeless eyes stared at the ceiling, her face contorted and mouth open. The room smelt of garlic. Althea looked around and located what she had expected to find, the open tin of marzipan.

"She ate her own poisoned candy," Althea said in a low voice. "I suppose there is some justice in that." She stood and addressed the crowd in the hall. "Please send word to the apothecary. She appears to have had an apoplectic fit. There is nothing more that can be done here tonight."

"My goodness!" said Lady Pickney. "And I thought nothing exciting ever happened in the country. What news shall I have to tell when word of tonight's business gets out! Two dead in one summer!"

Althea looked back at Mr. Gregson curled up on the floor, and felt a rush of pity. "No, Lady Pickney, you will not spread this tidbit of gossip, if you please. I think that this matter would be best handled quietly for all of the parties concerned, including our wonderful host. Promise me your discretion, and I will give you an even better piece of news."

Lady Pickney hesitated a moment, as if considering the matter, and then sighed. "Well, I suppose you are right. It is a bit sordid, after all. So what is this exciting news?"

Norwich stood and addressed the crowd, "Only that Lady Trent has consented to be my wife, and we shall be married as soon as may be arranged."

Lady Pickney clapped her hands together. "Oh, I knew it! How exciting! And to think I was here to witness it! All the London biddies will be so jealous. You have no idea."

CHAPTER TWENTY-SEVEN

Althea sat at her desk in the library, looking out through
the window to her right, over the lawn to the copse of
trees. Her son Arthur was happily at play with several of the
spaniel puppies recently delivered of Buttons, the dog that
was a descendant of a spaniel originally given to her by her
father. She should have been attending to her business – the
most exclusive wedding the area had seen was only a week
away – and there was much left to do.

At least, the initial meeting between Norwich and her
son had been got through without incident. Norwich had
made an effort to be agreeable. He had brought with him
a gift of a new translation of the *Odyssey,* which was immediately accepted with pleasure. Althea, who knew her son
better than anyone, had some hope that, after this initial
promising meeting, Arthur would come to esteem and perhaps even love him.

Norwich's mother had taken the news of the engagement with a wary amount of joy. It was clear, however, that the location of the ceremony left much to be desired. While she never went so far as to criticize Dettamoor Park in Althea's hearing, her looks of disdain gave her away. This made Althea surmise that Norwich had not seen fit to explain to his mother the exact provenance of his new bride. If the wife of a baronet were not good enough for her son, then the daughter of a physician certainly would not meet with the duchess' approbation. As Althea didn't feel that the qualms of the mother were enough to dissuade her from marrying the son, she tried to put it out of her mind and hope for the best.

Althea gathered her papers and set her mind back to work. She had to finish these accounts for the estate and then make sure that her affairs were in order before she and Norwich married. There were the documents from the lawyer to review. It was amazing how many documents a simple marriage could generate when there were property and estates on both sides. Her marriage to Sir Arthur had not been about anything but his desire to share in their mutual love of science. It was only later, when illness showed Sir Arthur his mortality, that lawyers had been brought in to document the terms of wedded bliss.

There was a knock at the half open door, and she looked up to see Norwich standing on the threshold, holding some papers in one hand and a small box in the other. Her heart did a strange counter beat.

"Are you much occupied at the moment?" he said.

"Nothing that cannot be interrupted." She held up some sheaves of paper. "Just my accounts."

"Surely someone else can assist you with those."

"As much as I love Jane, she has never had a head for figures, and someone must take the reins of the management until my son comes of age."

"Then perhaps these will be of interest. I took the liberty of abstracting the letters from the footman in order to have an excuse to come and see you." He closed the door behind him and held the letters out to her.

Althea stepped out from behind her desk and came towards him. "I hope that an excuse was not necessary."

"As you have required my entire family to join us here as a measure against impropriety, I am reduced to the basest forms of subterfuge." He handed her the letters, but, retaining her arm, leaned down to kiss her.

She kissed him back, and would have spent several more minutes thus pleasurably engaged had the clock not struck two and recalled her to her duty. She withdrew reluctantly. "I should review my correspondence."

He let her go. "At least one of us has the willpower to resist temptation. I have never felt the time drag on as it does until our wedding." His voice dipped lower, so as not to be heard beyond the door. "Or more correctly, our wedding night."

Althea looked hurriedly down at her letters so as not to betray the tumult of her emotions. "Ah, here is one from Mr. Read." She opened it and then quickly scanned his scratchy penmanship. She looked up suddenly and regarded Norwich. "She did not confess."

"Who?"

"Mrs. Gregson. She refused to speak to the magistrate before she took her own life and so the only account of the case was what I relayed to him. And as she is no longer alive to confirm or deny it, they have closed the matter entirely. The new Lord Tunwell is not to know of his parentage or how he came into his inheritance."

"I am sure that was her intent all along. It was her last selfless act on his behalf. I hope, for her sake, that he begins to live in a different style than he did before."

"Do you think he would be more likely to change if he knew the whole?" she said.

"No, the less said to him, the better. He must never know that he is not the true Lord Tunwell."

"And yet —"

"Althea, my love, if you fret over that man's fate any longer, I shall begin to think you had rather marry him."

"No, of course not, sorry." She looked back at her letters.

"Besides, I have something I wish to give you. I know that I should have produced it long ago, but I didn't think you would be willing to marry me before the lapse of six months and so —"

Althea cut him off. "Oh my lord, how delightful. They have accepted it!"

"What?"

"The monograph on the classification of the properties of soil to be used in the detection of criminal activity! You see, every soil is different and can be classified according to its appearance. Therefore, clothing or shoes will pick up soil, and then the scientist may determine where the person has been. The Royal Society! Only think. Here Lord Aldridge says that the work presents another novel approach!" She thrust the paper at him.

He took it and scanned it and then handed it back to her, his face suddenly hard. "When were you planning to tell me that you were publishing your own work under the name of your late husband?"

His question caught her up short. "How do you know that this is not Arthur's work?" she said defiantly.

"Because you have now published two monographs on the subject of criminal detection, and I cannot find from any of the persons here that Sir Arthur was involved with criminal detection in any form or fashion other than to peruse the *Hue and Cry* at his leisure when it was delivered to the house. Was he involved in fighting crime?"

"No, not precisely."

"Whereas you have done nothing but involve yourself in one crime after another the whole of our acquaintance."

"Well, yes, but it was the only way I could get my work published. In case you didn't know it, the Royal Society does not accept women, no matter what their merit!"

Norwich looked at her as if seeing her for the first time. "This can't go on."

Althea pulled herself up to her full height. "I will not give up my work. If you cannot stomach the idea of a lady scientist, then I do not see that we can ever marry."

There was a pregnant pause, and Althea felt her heart skip a beat.

Norwich took a deep breath and replied. "No, you misunderstand me. This can't go on because you cannot live in your deceased husband's shadow. It is not right. And I don't like secrets between us. After everything we have endured, you should have trusted me."

Althea relaxed. "I am sorry. All my life, I have longed to achieve great things in the world of science, only to be trapped by my gender. I didn't think you would comprehend my predicament."

"I do." He held out the box to her. "And I know that for you these will pale in comparison to Aldridge's gift of a published monograph, but I thought you should have them just the same. They are my betrothal gift to you."

Althea looked at him with wonder. Truth be told, she had not thought about betrothal gifts in the rush of planning and organizing required to host a double wedding.

She cautiously took the box and opened it. There, on the bed of velvet, lay a pair of emerald earrings and a matching bracelet. "Why, these are like the ones you gave me to catch the Richmond Thief!"

"They were my grandmother's and her mother's before her. I had them copied for you to catch a thief, but these are the real gems."

"Oh my. I don't know what to say. Are you sure your family would approve?"

He smiled. "What can they say? Besides," he gently clasped the bracelet around her wrist. "after that first stolen kiss, I could never look upon them without thinking of you."

Althea looked down at the bracelet on her wrist. She realized that she had given little thought to what her life would be like as a duchess, and not merely the widow of a country baronet. The weight of that uncertainty suddenly hit her hard. She took a deep breath to steady her nerves and looked up. Norwich's eyes held such an expression of warmth and affection – it was more than she ever dreamed possible in her contemplation of the future. She would worry about her new life later. "I do love you," she said.

"And I love you, my dearest, loveliest, most brilliant, Althea."

ACKNOWLEDGMENTS

I would like to thank my family, especially my mother, for support and guidance. Dara, Cindy and Kajal also deserve recognition for their editorial assistance. Thanks also to my book group, viewers of Marshfield TV, and the fans around the country who have made **The Richmond Thief** such a success. And finally, I want to thank my colleagues and friends at Security Health Plan for their continued support of my writing career.

ABOUT THE AUTHOR

Lisa Boero is a lawyer and moonlighting novelist. She is the author of the **Nerdy Girls** series of mysteries, featuring face-blind detective Liz Howe. Boero's third book, **Hell Made Easy**, is a dark comedy about lawyers in a battle of wits with the devil. **The Richmond Thief** and **The Ranleigh Question**, which follow the trials of the indomitable Lady Althea, are the product of the author's infatuation with Jane Austen and the **Forensic Files**.

Boero lives in Marshfield, Wisconsin, along with her family, and can be contacted at www.lisaboero.com.